Cast of Characters

MIKHAIL IVANOFF KOSTILYOFF, *keeper of a night lodging.*
VASSILISA KARPOVNA, *his wife.*
NATASHA, *her sister.*
MIEDVIEDIEFF, *her uncle, a policeman.*
VASKA PEPEL, *a young thief.*
ANDREI MITRITCH KLESHTCH, *a locksmith.*
ANNA, *his wife.*
NASTYA, *a street-walker.*
KVASHNYA, *a vendor of meat-pies.*
BUBNOFF, *a cap-maker.*
THE BARON.
SATINE.
THE ACTOR.
LUKA, *a pilgrim.*
ALYOSHKA, *a shoemaker.*
KRIVOY ZOB ⎫
               ⎬ *Porters.*
THE TARTAR ⎭
NIGHT LODGERS, TRAMPS AND OTHERS.

*The action takes place in a night lodging and in
"The Waste," an area in its rear.*

DOVER · THRIFT · EDITIONS

The Lower Depths

MAXIM GORKY

TRANSLATED BY
JENNIE COVAN

DOVER PUBLICATIONS, INC.
Mineola, New York

DOVER THRIFT EDITIONS

GENERAL EDITOR: PAUL NEGRI

EDITOR OF THIS VOLUME: JULIE NORD

Theatrical Rights

This Dover Thrift Edition may be used in its entirety, in adaptation, or in any other way for theatrical productions, professional and amateur, in the United States, without fee, permission, or acknowledgment. (This may not apply outside of the United States, as copyright conditions may vary.)

Bibliographical Note

This Dover edition, first published in 2000, is an unabridged republication of the Jennie Covan translation of Maxim Gorky's *The Lower Depths*, first published in 1923 by Brentano's Publishers, New York. A new introductory Note has been specially prepared for this edition.

Library of Congress Cataloging-in-Publication Data

Gorky, Maksim, 1868–1936.
    [Na dne. English]
    The lower depths / Maxim Gorky ; translated by Jennie Covan.
       p. cm. — (Dover thrift editions)
    Originally published: New York : Brentano's, 1923.
    ISBN 0-486-41115-X (pbk.)
     I. Covan, Jenny. II. Title. III. Series.

PG3463.N2 C6 2000
891.72'3—dc21

99-054723

Manufactured in the United States of America
Dover Publications, Inc., 31 East 2nd Street, Mineola, N.Y. 11501

Note

MAXIM GORKY was born Alexey Maximovich Peshkov in 1868 in Nizhni-Novgorod. At the age of 24, upon the publication of his first story, he adopted the name "Gorky," which means "bitter" (his hometown later adopted it as well, in his honor). His early life explains his choice: When Gorky was just five his father died and he was sent to live with his maternal grandparents. His grandmother was kind and jovial, but his grandfather was a harsh, often brutal man at the low point in his own fortunes and therefore at his angriest while Gorky lived with him. The boy's own parents had never hit him, but the first beating he received from his grandfather left him unconscious, and then bed-ridden for weeks. Thereafter, beatings and displays of egregious cruelty were commonplace in his life, as they were for his grandmother, his aunts, his cousins—nearly everyone he knew. His male relatives were usually the perpetrators, and often they were violent amongst themselves as well. And so he was plunged into a world of desperation and pain in which the strong compulsively brutalized the weak and the weak simply clung to their lives by any sad means they knew.

Gorky attended school briefly, but preferred to spend his time on the streets with his friends. By the age of eleven, he was already an experienced thief. His grandfather, now thoroughly destitute, sent Gorky out to work and from then on the boy was to move from job to job—errand boy, dish washer, printer's devil—experiencing what clearly seemed every form of confinement, exploitation, and degradation imaginable. He was frequently beaten, underfed, ill clothed. The ordeal very nearly finished him, yet along the way he was learning more and more about the characters and the predicaments that would make his writings so powerful and ground-breaking. He was also discovering the world of books, which became his great passion: "Like some wondrous birds out of fairy tales, books sang their songs to me and spoke to me as though communing with one languishing in prison. . . . Each book was a rung in my ascent from the brutish to the human, towards an understanding of a better life and a thirst after that life." Still, a life of unremitting misery stretched before him and there were no easy ways out. When he was nineteen his despair drove him to an unsuccessful suicide attempt, which left a bullet in his lung that eventually hastened his 1936 death by tuberculosis.

Still, Gorky continued to read, study and write, and in 1892, having truly earned his pseudonym, he began to publish the stories, plays and journalism that were to turn him into the literary hero of his generation. His tales of hopeless lives and his jaded, world-weary characters were passionately embraced by his peers, people who had never before seen their existence validated in letters. Stefan Zweig wrote, "The effect of Gorky's first works was indescribably portentous, like an upheaval, an alarm, a wrench, a breaking . . . a different Russia from that of the past had here spoken for the first time, [and] this voice came from the gigantic, anguished breast of a whole people."

Gorky's rise to literary fame became inextricably linked to the liberation of the Russian people from the imperial order. In time, his was the body of work that came to define Socialist Realism, while the role of "father of Socialist Realism" came to define Gorky in a way that was not always accurate or to his advantage. Although he was always committed to political struggle and revolutionary inclinations, and although he was a life-long friend of Lenin's, he frequently attacked the "party line"—to Lenin's great distress. In fact, Gorky often published his arguments against Lenin's programs, so that in time, Lenin saw fit to shut down Gorky's newspaper and eventually all of his dissenting publications were expunged from "official" catalogues of his works.

The Lower Depths, written in 1902 and produced that same year at the Moscow Art Theatre under the direction of Stanislavsky, was an enormous and immediate success. Even before its premiere, the great dramatist Chekhov had written Gorky to say, "I have read your play. It is new and unmistakably fine. The second act is . . . the best, the strongest, and when I was reading it . . . I almost danced with joy." It is reported that Gorky received 22 curtain calls at the opening, and the reviews were all praise.

Infinite pains were taken by both director and cast to render all the details of life "At the Bottom" (which is a more precise English equivalent of Gorky's title, *Na dne*) as realistically as possible, and to determine the manner in which Gorky's speeches should be delivered: "Our natures were alien to Gorky's wide gestures, to his revelatory thoughts, to his sharp aphorisms, to his destructive flights, and to his peculiar pathos," Stanislavsky later wrote. "One must be able to say Gorky's words so that the phrases live and resound. The instructive and propagandistic speeches of Gorky . . . must be pronounced simply and with sincere enthusiasm, without any false and highfalutin theatricality.

Otherwise a serious play will become a mere melodrama." This realism was integral to the Moscow Art Theatre's mission. Oliver M. Sayler, editor of *Moscow Art Theatre Plays* (1923), wrote

> In "The Lower Depths" more than in any other single play throughout its history, the Moscow Art Theatre . . . most emphatically justifies its artistic faith in spiritual or psychological realism as a dramatic means of expression. . . . Less than any play I know, is it possible to imagine its potential effect in the theatre from a reading of its printed lines. . . ."The Lower Depths" is not so much a matter of utterable line and recountable gesture as it is of the intangible flow of human souls in endlessly shifting contact with one another. Awkward but eloquent pauses and emphases, the scarcely perceptible stress or dulling of word or gesture, the nuances and the shadings of which life is mostly made and by which it reveals its meaning—these . . . are the incalculable and unrecorded channels through which "The Lower Depths" becomes articulate . . .

For decades, this drama was held up as an indictment of the tsarist regime and its immense popularity was partially due to that assessment of its intent. Later scholarship has pointed out, however, that nothing in the play itself supports this view, that the bleak situation of the play's characters is presented as resulting from their own failures or some malevolent trick of fate. Indeed, Gorky's most urgent concern seems to be, not who's to blame for the misery of the lost souls who inhabit Kostilyoff's night lodging (the play's setting), but whether and how any of them might find release.

It is a concern that also drives Gorky's three-volume autobiography, and the characters that populate that work often seem to find their voices in those of *The Lower Depths*. Gorky's grandmother, aunts, and mother—all the women he knew who bore their husbands' violence in silence—seem to speak through Anna, whose husband's beatings have left her so weak and ill that her only hope is death. Luka the pilgrim recalls another side of Gorky's grandmother: the ever-faithful, pure-hearted side, full of affection, hope, and enchanting stories which provided a constant escape valve for both her and young Gorky. Nastya, the young prostitute who finds her escape in sentimental romance novels, reminds us of the adolescent Gorky, forced into work he found sordid and demeaning yet clinging to the dream-like worlds he was discovering in books. Pepel, the young thief in love, resembles the pre-adolescent Gorky who fell into a life of petty crime partly out of resentment and anger and partly out of ignorance—simply not knowing any other way to go. Each of these characters, and Gorky himself, can be seen as struggling to discover anything at all—God? Love? Work? Learning?—that is worthy of their faith.

Gorky once wrote "I am a very dubious Marxist . . . I do not have any

faith in the intelligence of the masses in general." As a child, he had
found solace in his grandmother's religion. Later in life, though no
longer a Christian, he sought continually after a connection to something mystical, to some type of faith that would recapture the sense of
hope that the church had once offered. As he was to write many times,
what Gorky did believe in was "Man," and his life and work were ded-
icated to plumbing the truth about humanity—What is our purpose?
What are we, finally, longing for? Why do we hang on to life, despite
its pain?

Gorky's answer seems to lie, at least in part, in Satine's Act IV
speech:

> Every one . . . lives in the hope of something better. That's why we
> must respect each and every human being! How do we know who he is,
> why he was born, and what he is capable of accomplishing? Perhaps his
> coming into the world will prove to be our good fortune . . . Especially
> must we respect little children! Children—need freedom! Don't inter-
> fere with their lives! Respect children!

This plea surely speaks directly out of Gorky's own childhood. It is an
injunction directed towards all of humanity to protect other children
from witnessing, from living, the sort of hopeless existence he endured
and then faithfully captured in *The Lower Depths*; his brave effort, perhaps, to send such tales into permanent exile, from the realm of human
experience to the realm of the theater.

The Lower Depths

Contents

Act I

A cellar resembling a cave. The ceiling, which merges into stone walls, is
  low and grimy, and the plaster and paint are peeling off. There is
  a window, high up on the right wall, from which comes the light.
  The right corner, which constitutes Pepel's room, is partitioned off
  by thin boards. Close to the corner of this room is Bubnoff's wooden
  bunk. In the left corner stands a large Russian stove. In the stone
  wall, left, is a door leading to the kitchen where live Kvashnya, the
  Baron, and Nastya. Against the wall, between the stove and the
  door, is a large bed covered with dirty chintz. Bunks line the walls.
  In the foreground, by the left wall, is a block of wood with a vise
  and a small anvil fastened to it, and another smaller block of wood
  somewhat further towards the back. Kleshtch is seated on the
  smaller block, trying keys into old locks. At his feet are two large
  bundles of various keys, wired together, also a battered tin samovar,
  a hammer and pincers. In the centre are a large table, two
  benches, and a stool, all of which are of dirty, unpainted wood.
  Behind the table Kvashnya is busying herself with the samovar. The
  Baron sits chewing a piece of black bread, and Nastya occupies the
  stool, leans her elbows on the table, and reads a tattered book. In
  the bed, behind curtains, Anna lies coughing. Bubnoff is seated on
  his bunk, attempting to shape a pair of old trousers with the help
  of an ancient hat shape, which he holds between his knees.
  Scattered about him are pieces of buckram, oilcloth, and rags.
  Satine, just awakened, lies in his bunk, grunting. On top of the
  stove, the Actor, invisible to the audience, tosses about and coughs.
It is an early spring morning.

THE BARON.   And then?
KVASHNYA.   No, my dear, said I, keep away from me with such pro-
posals. I've been through it all, you see—and not for a hundred baked
lobsters would I marry again!

1

BUBNOFF [*to* SATINE].   What are you grunting about? [SATINE *keeps on grunting*]

KVASHNYA.   Why should I, said I, a free woman, my own mistress, enter my name into somebody else's passport and sell myself into slavery—no! Why—I wouldn't marry a man even if he were an American prince!

KLESHTCH.   You lie!

KVASHNYA.   Wha-at?

KLESHTCH.   You lie! You're going to marry Abramka. . . .

THE BARON [*snatching the book out of* NASTYA's *hand and reading the title*].   "Fatal Love" . . . [*Laughs*]

NASTYA [*stretching out her hand*].   Give it back—give it back! Stop fooling!

[THE BARON *looks at her and waves the book in the air.*]

KVASHNYA [*to* KLESHTCH].   You crimson goat, you—calling me a liar! How dare you be so rude to me?

THE BARON [*hitting* NASTYA *on the head with the book*].   Nastya, you little fool!

NASTYA [*reaching for the book*].   Give it back!

KLESHTCH.   Oh—what a great lady . . . but you'll marry Abramka just the same—that's all you're waiting for . . .

KVASHNYA.   Sure! Anything else? You nearly beat your wife to death!

KLESHTCH.   Shut up, you old bitch! It's none of your business!

KVASHNYA.   Ho-ho! can't stand the truth, can you?

THE BARON.   They're off again! Nastya, where are you?

NASTYA [*without lifting her head*].   Hey—go away!

ANNA [*putting her head through the curtains*].   The day has started. For God's sake, don't row!

KLESHTCH.   Whining again!

ANNA.   Every blessed day . . . let me die in peace, can't you?

BUBNOFF.   Noise won't keep you from dying.

KVASHNYA [*walking up to* ANNA].   Little mother, how did you ever manage to live with this wretch?

ANNA.   Leave me alone—get away from me. . . .

KVASHNYA.   Well, well! You poor soul . . . how's the pain in the chest—any better?

THE BARON.   Kvashnya! Time to go to market. . . .

KVASHNYA.   We'll go presently. [*To* ANNA] Like some hot dumplings?

ANNA.   No, thanks. Why should I eat?

KVASHNYA.   You must eat. Hot food—good for you! I'll leave you some in a cup. Eat them when you feel like it. Come on, sir! [*To* KLESHTCH] You evil spirit! [*Goes into kitchen*]

ANNA [*coughing*].   Lord, Lord . . .

THE BARON [*painfully pushing forward* NASTYA's *head*].   Throw it away—little fool!

NASTYA [*muttering*].   Leave me alone—I don't bother you . . .

[THE BARON *follows* KVASHNYA, *whistling.*]

SATINE [*sitting up in his bunk*].   Who beat me up yesterday?

BUBNOFF.   Does it make any difference who?

SATINE.   Suppose they did—but why did they?

BUBNOFF.   Were you playing cards?

SATINE.   Yes!

BUBNOFF.   That's why they beat you.

SATINE.   Scoundrels!

THE ACTOR [*raising his head from the top of the stove*].   One of these days they'll beat you to death!

SATINE.   You're a jackass!

THE ACTOR.   Why?

SATINE.   Because a man can die only once!

THE ACTOR [*after a silence*].   I don't understand—

KLESHTCH.   Say! You crawl from that stove—and start cleaning house! Don't play the delicate primrose!

THE ACTOR.   None of your business!

KLESHTCH.   Wait till Vassilisa comes—she'll show you whose business it is!

THE ACTOR.   To hell with Vassilisa! To-day is the Baron's turn to clean. . . . Baron!

[THE BARON *comes from the kitchen.*]

THE BARON.   I've no time to clean . . . I'm going to market with Kvashnya.

THE ACTOR.   That doesn't concern me. Go to the gallows if you like. It's your turn to sweep the floor just the same—I'm not going to do other people's work . . .

THE BARON.   Go to blazes! Nastya will do it. Hey there—fatal love! Wake up! [*Takes the book away from* NASTYA]

NASTYA [*getting up*].   What do you want? Give it back to me! You scoundrel! And that's a nobleman for you!

THE BARON [*returning the book to her*].   Nastya! Sweep the floor for me—will you?

NASTYA [*goes to kitchen*].   Not so's you'll notice it!

KVASHNYA [*to* THE BARON *through kitchen door*].   Come on—you!

They don't need you! Actor! You were asked to do it, and now you go
ahead and attend to it—it won't kill you . . .

THE ACTOR.   It's always I . . . I don't understand why. . . .

[THE BARON *comes from the kitchen, across his shoulders a wooden
beam from which hang earthen pots covered with rags.*]

THE BARON.   Heavier than ever!

SATINE.   It paid you to be born a Baron, eh?

KVASHNYA [*to* ACTOR].   See to it that you sweep up! [*Crosses to outer
door, letting* THE BARON *pass ahead*]

THE ACTOR [*climbing down from the stove*].   It's bad for me to inhale dust. [*With pride*] My organism is poisoned with alcohol. [*Sits
down on a bunk, meditating*]

SATINE.   Organism—organon. . . .

ANNA.   Andrei Mitritch. . . .

KLESHTCH.   What now?

ANNA.   Kvashnya left me some dumplings over there—you eat
them!

KLESHTCH [*coming over to her*].   And you—don't you want any?

ANNA.   No. Why should I eat? You're a workman—you need it.

KLESHTCH.   Frightened, are you? Don't be! You'll get all right!

ANNA.   Go and eat! It's hard on me. . . . I suppose very soon . . .

KLESHTCH [*walking away*].   Never mind—maybe you'll get well—
you can never tell! [*Goes into kitchen*]

THE ACTOR [*loud, as if he had suddenly awakened*].   Yesterday the
doctor in the hospital said to me: "Your organism," he said, "is entirely
poisoned with alcohol . . ."

SATINE [*smiling*].   Organon . . .

THE ACTOR [*stubbornly*].   Not organon—organism!

SATINE.   Sibylline. . . .

THE ACTOR [*shaking his fist at him*]:   Nonsense! I'm telling you se-
riously . . . if the organism is poisoned . . . that means it's bad for me to
sweep the floor—to inhale the dust . . .

SATINE.   Macrobistic . . . hah!

BUBNOFF.   What are you muttering?

SATINE.   Words—and here's another one for you—transcendental-
istic . . .

BUBNOFF.   What does it mean?

SATINE.   Don't know—I forgot . . .

BUBNOFF.   Then why did you say it?

SATINE.   Just so! I'm bored, brother, with human words—all our
words. Bored! I've heard each one of them a thousand times surely.

THE ACTOR.   In Hamlet they say: "Words, words, words!" It's a good play. I played the grave-digger in it once. . . .

[KLESHTCH *comes from the kitchen.*]

KLESHTCH.   Will you start playing with the broom?
THE ACTOR.   None of your business. [*Striking his chest*] Ophelia! O—remember me in thy prayers!

[*Backstage is heard a dull murmur, cries, and a police whistle.* KLESHTCH *sits down to work, filing screechily.*]

SATINE.   I love unintelligible, obsolete words. When I was a youngster—and worked as a telegraph operator—I read heaps of books. . . .
BUBNOFF.   Were you really a telegrapher?
SATINE.   I was. There are some excellent books—and lots of curious words . . . Once I was an educated man, do you know?
BUBNOFF.   I've heard it a hundred times. Well, so you were! That isn't very important! Me—well—once I was a furrier. I had my own shop—what with dyeing the fur all day long, my arms were yellow up to the elbows, brother. I thought I'd never be able ever to get clean again—that I'd go to my grave, all yellow! But look at my hands now—they're plain dirty—that's what!
SATINE.   Well, and what then?
BUBNOFF.   That's all!
SATINE.   What are you trying to prove?
BUBNOFF.   Oh, well—just matching thoughts—no matter how much dye you get on yourself, it all comes off in the end—yes, yes—
SATINE.   Oh—my bones ache!
THE ACTOR [*sits, nursing his knees*].   Education is all rot. Talent is the thing. I knew an actor—who read his parts by heart, syllable by syllable—but he played heroes in a way that . . . why—the whole theatre would rock with ecstasy!
SATINE.   Bubnoff, give me five kopecks.
BUBNOFF.   I only have two—
THE ACTOR.   I say—talent, that's what you need to play heroes. And talent is nothing but faith in yourself, in your own powers—
SATINE.   Give me five kopecks and I'll have faith that you're a hero, a crocodile, or a police inspector—Kleshtch, give me five kopecks.
KLESHTCH.   Go to hell! All of you!
SATINE.   What are you cursing for? I know you haven't a kopeck in the world!
ANNA.   Andrei Mitritch—I'm suffocating—I can't breathe—
KLESHTCH.   What shall I do?
BUBNOFF.   Open the door into the hall.

KLESHTCH.   All right. You're sitting on the bunk, I on the floor. You change places with me, and I'll let you open the door. I have a cold as it is.

BUBNOFF [*unconcernedly*].   I don't care if you open the door—it's your wife who's asking—

KLESHTCH [*morosely*].   I don't care who's asking—

SATINE.   My head buzzes—ah—why do people have to hit each other over the heads?

BUBNOFF.   They don't only hit you over the head, but over the rest of the body as well. [*Rises*] I must go and buy some thread—our bosses are late to-day—seems as if they've croaked. [*Exits*]

[ANNA *coughs;* SATINE *is lying down motionless, his hands folded behind his head.*]

THE ACTOR [*looks about him morosely, then goes to* ANNA].   Feeling bad, eh?

ANNA.   I'm choking—

THE ACTOR.   If you wish, I'll take you into the hallway. Get up, then, come! [*He helps her to rise, wraps some sort of a rag about her shoulders, and supports her toward the hall*] It isn't easy. I'm sick myself—poisoned with alcohol . . .

[KOSTILYOFF *appears in the doorway.*]

KOSTILYOFF.   Going for a stroll? What a nice couple—the gallant cavalier and the lady fair!

THE ACTOR.   Step aside, you—don't you see that we're invalids?

KOSTILYOFF.   Pass on, please! [*Hums a religious tune, glances about him suspiciously, and bends his head to the left as if listening to what is happening in* PEPEL's *room.* KLESHTCH *is jangling his keys and scraping away with his file, and looks askance at the other*] Filing?

KLESHTCH.   What?

KOSTILYOFF.   I say, are you filing? [*Pause*] What did I want to ask? [*Quick and low*] Hasn't my wife been here?

KLESHTCH.   I didn't see her.

KOSTILYOFF [*carefully moving toward* PEPEL's *room*]. You take up a whole lot of room for your two rubles a month. The bed—and your bench—yes—you take up five rubles' worth of space, so help me God! I'll have to put another half ruble to your rent—

KLESHTCH.   You'll put a noose around my neck and choke me . . . you'll croak soon enough, and still all you think of is half rubles—

KOSTILYOFF.   Why should I choke you? What would be the use? God be with you—live and prosper! But I'll have to raise you half a ruble—I'll buy oil for the ikon lamp, and my offering will atone for my sins, and for yours as well. You don't think much of your sins—not much! Oh, Andrushka, you're a wicked man! Your wife is dying because of your wickedness—no one loves you, no one respects you—your work is squeaky, jarring on every one.

KLESHTCH [shouts]. What do you come here for—just to annoy me?

[SATINE grunts loudly.]

KOSTILYOFF [with a start]. God, what a noise!

[THE ACTOR enters.]

THE ACTOR. I've put her down in the hall and wrapped her up.

KOSTILYOFF. You're a kindly fellow. That's good. Some day you'll be rewarded for it.

THE ACTOR. When?

KOSTILYOFF. In the Beyond, little brother—there all our deeds will be reckoned up.

THE ACTOR. Suppose you reward me right now?

KOSTILYOFF. How can I do that?

THE ACTOR. Wipe out half my debt.

KOSTILYOFF. He-ho! You're always jesting, darling—always poking fun . . . can kindliness of heart be repaid with gold? Kindliness—it's above all other qualities. But your debt to me—remains a debt. And so you'll have to pay me back. You ought to be kind to me, an old man, without seeking for reward!

THE ACTOR. You're a swindler, old man! [Goes into kitchen]

[KLESHTCH rises and goes into the hall.]

KOSTILYOFF [to SATINE]. See that squeaker—? He ran away—he doesn't like me!

SATINE. Does anybody like you besides the Devil?

KOSTILYOFF [laughing]. Oh—you're so quarrelsome! But I like you all—I understand you all, my unfortunate down-trodden, useless brethren . . . [Suddenly, rapidly] Is Vaska home?

SATINE. See for yourself—

KOSTILYOFF [goes to the door and knocks]. Vaska!

[THE ACTOR appears at the kitchen door, chewing something.]

PEPEL. Who is it?

KOSTILYOFF. It's I—I, Vaska!

PEPEL. What do you want?

KOSTILYOFF [stepping aside]. Open!

SATINE [*without looking at* KOSTILYOFF].   He'll open—and she's there—

[THE ACTOR *makes a grimace.*]

KOSTILYOFF [*in a low, anxious tone*].   Eh? Who's there? What?
SATINE.   Speaking to me?
KOSTILYOFF.   What did you say?
SATINE.   Oh—nothing—I was just talking to myself—
KOSTILYOFF.   Take care, brother. Don't carry your joking too far! [*Knocks loudly at door*] Vassily!
PEPEL [*opening door*].   Well? What are you disturbing me for?
KOSTILYOFF [*peering into room*].   I—you see—
PEPEL.   Did you bring the money?
KOSTILYOFF.   I've something to tell you—
PEPEL.   Did you bring the money?
KOSTILYOFF.   What money? Wait—
PEPEL.   Why—the seven rubles for the watch—well?
KOSTILYOFF.   What watch, Vaska? Oh, you—
PEPEL.   Look here. Yesterday, before witnesses, I sold you a watch for ten rubles, you gave me three—now let me have the other seven. What are you blinking for? You hang around here—you disturb people—and don't seem to know yourself what you're after.
KOSTILYOFF.   Sh-sh! Don't be angry, Vaska. The watch—it is—
SATINE.   Stolen!
KOSTILYOFF [*sternly*].   I do not accept stolen goods—how can you imagine—
PEPEL [*taking him by the shoulder*].   What did you disturb me for? What do you want?
KOSTILYOFF.   I don't want—anything. I'll go—if you're in such a state—
PEPEL.   Be off, and bring the money!
KOSTILYOFF.   What ruffians! I—I—[*Exits*]
THE ACTOR.   What a farce!
SATINE.   That's fine—I like it.
PEPEL.   What did he come here for?
SATINE [*laughing*].   Don't you understand? He's looking for his wife. Why don't you beat him up once and for all, Vaska?
PEPEL.   Why should I let such trash interfere with my life?
SATINE.   Show some brains! And then you can marry Vassilisa—and become our boss—
PEPEL.   Heavenly bliss! And you'd smash up my household and, because I'm a soft-hearted fool, you'll drink up everything I possess. [*Sits on a bunk*] Old devil—woke me up—I was having such a pleasant

dream. I dreamed I was fishing—and I caught an enormous trout—such a trout as you only see in dreams! I was playing him—and I was so afraid the line would snap. I had just got out the gaff—and I thought to myself—in a moment—

SATINE.   It wasn't a trout, it was Vassilisa—

THE ACTOR.   He caught Vassilisa a long time ago.

PEPEL [*angrily*].   You can all go to the devil—and Vassilisa with you—

[KLESHTCH *comes from the hall.*]

KLESHTCH.   Devilishly cold!

THE ACTOR.   Why didn't you bring Anna back? She'll freeze, out there—

KLESHTCH.   Natasha took her into the kitchen—

THE ACTOR.   The old man will kick her out—

KLESHTCH [*sitting down to his work*].   Well—Natasha will bring her in here—

SATINE.   Vassily—give me five kopecks!

THE ACTOR [*to* SATINE].   Oh, you—always five kopecks—Vassya—give us twenty kopecks—

PEPEL.   I'd better give it to them now before they ask for a ruble. Here you are!

SATINE.   Gibraltar! There are no kindlier people in the world than thieves!

KLESHTCH [*morosely*].   They earn their money easily—they don't work—

SATINE.   Many earn it easily, but not many part with it so easily. Work? Make work pleasant—and maybe I'll work too. Yes—maybe. When work's a pleasure, life's, too. When it's toil, then life is a drudge. [*To* THE ACTOR] You, Sardanapalus! Come on!

THE ACTOR.   Let's go, Nebuchadnezzar! I'll get as drunk as forty thousand topers!

[*They leave.*]

PEPEL [*yawning*].   Well, how's your wife?

KLESHTCH.   It seems as if soon—[*Pause*]

PEPEL.   Now I look at you—seems to me all that filing and scraping of yours is useless.

KLESHTCH.   Well—what else can I do?

PEPEL.   Nothing.

KLESHTCH.   How can I live?

PEPEL.   People manage, somehow.

KLESHTCH.   Them? Call them people? Muck and dregs—that's

what they are! I'm a workman—I'm ashamed even to look at them. I've
slaved since I was a child. . . . D'you think I shan't be able to tear myself away from here? I'll crawl out of here, even if I have to leave my
skin behind—but crawl out I will! Just wait . . . my wife'll die . . . I've
lived here six months, and it seems like six years.

PEPEL.   Nobody here's any worse off than you . . . say what you
like . . .

KLESHTCH.   No worse is right. They've neither honor nor conscience.

PEPEL [*indifferently*].   What good does it do—honor or conscience?
Can you get them on their feet instead of on their uppers—through
honor and conscience? Honor and conscience are needed only by
those who have power and energy . . .

BUBNOFF [*coming back*].   Oh—I'm frozen . . .

PEPEL.   Bubnoff! Got a conscience?

BUBNOFF.   What? A conscience?

PEPEL.   Exactly!

BUBNOFF.   What do I need a conscience for? I'm not rich.

PEPEL.   Just what I said: honor and conscience are for the rich—
right! And Kleshtch is upbraiding us because we haven't any!

BUBNOFF.   Why—did he want to borrow some of it?

PEPEL.   No—he has plenty of his own . . .

BUBNOFF.   Oh—are you selling it? You won't sell much around
here. But if you had some old boxes, I'd buy them—on credit . . .

PEPEL [*didactically*].   You're a jackass, Andrushka! On the subject
of conscience you ought to hear Satine—or the Baron . . .

KLESHTCH.   I've nothing to talk to them about!

PEPEL.   They have more brains than you—even if they're drunkards . . .

BUBNOFF.   He who can be drunk and wise at the same time is dou-
bly blessed . . .

PEPEL.   Satine says every man expects his neighbor to have a conscience, but—you see—it isn't to any one's advantage to have one—
that's a fact.

> [NATASHA *enters, followed by* LUKA *who carries a stick in his
> hand, a bundle on his back, a kettle and a teapot slung from
> his belt.*]

LUKA.   How are you, honest folks?

PEPEL [*twisting his mustache*].   Aha—Natasha!

BUBNOFF [*to* LUKA].   I was honest—up to spring before last.

NATASHA.   Here's a new lodger . . .

LUKA.   Oh, it's all the same to me. Crooks—I don't mind them, either. For my part there's no bad flea—they're all black—and they all jump . . . Well, dearie, show me where I can stow myself.

NATASHA [*pointing to kitchen door*].   Go in there, grand-dad.

LUKA.   Thanks, girlie! One place is like another—as long as an old fellow keeps warm, he keeps happy . . .

PEPEL.   What an amusing old codger you brought in, Natasha!

NATASHA.   A hanged sight more interesting than you! . . . Andrei, your wife's in the kitchen with us—come and fetch her after a while . . .

KLESHTCH.   All right—I will . . .

NATASHA.   And be a little more kind to her—you know she won't last much longer.

KLESHTCH. . I know . . .

NATASHA.   Knowing won't do any good—it's terrible—dying—don't you understand?

PEPEL.   Well—look at me—I'm not afraid . . .

NATASHA.   Oh—you're a wonder, aren't you?

BUBNOFF [*whistling*].   Oh—this thread's rotten . . .

PEPEL.   Honestly, I'm not afraid! I'm ready to die right now. Knife me to the heart—and I'll die without making a sound . . . even gladly—from such a pure hand . . .

NATASHA [*going out*].   Spin that yarn for some one else!

BUBNOFF.   Oh—that thread is rotten—rotten—

NATASHA [*at hallway door*].   Don't forget your wife, Andrei!

KLESHTCH.   All right.

PEPEL.   She's a wonderful girl!

BUBNOFF.   She's all right.

PEPEL.   What makes her so curt with me? Anyway—she'll come to no good here . . .

BUBNOFF.   Through you—sure!

PEPEL.   Why through me? I feel sorry for her . . .

BUBNOFF.   As the wolf for the lamb!

PEPEL.   You lie! I feel very sorry for her . . . very . . . very sorry! She has a tough life here—I can see that . . .

KLESHTCH.   Just wait till Vassilisa catches you talking to her!

BUBNOFF.   Vassilisa? She won't give up so easily what belongs to her—she's a cruel woman!

PEPEL [*stretching himself on the bunk*].   You two prophets can go to hell!

KLESHTCH.   Just wait—you'll see!

LUKA [*singing in the kitchen*].   "In the dark of the night the way is black . . ."

KLESHTCH.   Another one who yelps!

PEPEL.   It's dreary! Why do I feel so dreary? You live—and everything seems all right. But suddenly a cold chill goes through you—and then everything gets dreary . . .

BUBNOFF.   Dreary? Hm-hm—

PEPEL.   Yes—yes—

LUKA [*sings*].   "The way is black . . ."

PEPEL.   Old fellow! Hey there!

LUKA [*looking from kitchen door*].   You call me?

PEPEL.   Yes. Don't sing!

LUKA [*coming in*].   You don't like it?

PEPEL.   When people sing well I like it—

LUKA.   In other words—I don't sing well?

PEPEL.   Evidently!

LUKA.   Well, well—and I thought I sang well. That's always the way: a man imagines there's one thing he can do well, and suddenly he finds out that other people don't think so . . .

PEPEL [*laughs*].   That's right . . .

BUBNOFF.   First you say you feel dreary—and then you laugh!

PEPEL.   None of your business, raven!

LUKA.   Who do they say feels dreary?

PEPEL.   I do.

[THE BARON *enters.*]

LUKA.   Well, well—out there in the kitchen there's a girl reading and crying! That's so! Her eyes are wet with tears . . . I say to her: "What's the matter, darling?" And she says: "It's so sad!" "What's so sad?" say I. "The book!" says she.—And that's how people spend their time. Just because they're bored . . .

THE BARON.   She's a fool!

PEPEL.   Have you had tea, Baron?

THE BARON.   Yes. Go on!

PEPEL.   Well—want me to open a bottle?

THE BARON.   Of course. Go on!

PEPEL.   Drop on all fours, and bark like a dog!

THE BARON.   Fool! What's the matter with you? Are you drunk?

PEPEL.   Go on—bark a little! It'll amuse me. You're an aristocrat. You didn't even consider us human formerly, did you?

THE BARON.   Go on!

PEPEL.   Well—and now I am making you bark like a dog—and you will bark, won't you?

THE BARON.   All right. I will. You jackass! What pleasure can you derive from it since I myself know that I have sunk almost lower than you? You should have made me drop on all fours in the days when I was still above you.

BUBNOFF.   That's right . . .

LUKA.   I say so, too!

BUBNOFF.   What's over, is over. Remain only trivialities. We know no class distinctions here. We've shed all pride and self-respect. Blood and bone—man—just plain man—that's what we are!

LUKA.   In other words, we're all equal . . . and you, friend, were you really a Baron?

THE BARON.   Who are you? A ghost?

LUKA [*laughing*].   I've seen counts and princes in my day—this is the first time I meet a baron—and one who's decaying—at that!

PEPEL [*laughing*].   Baron, I blush for you!

THE BARON.   It's time you knew better, Vassily . . .

LUKA.   Hey-hey—I look at you, brothers—the life you're leading . . .

BUBNOFF.   Such a life! As soon as the sun rises, our voices rise, too—in quarrels!

THE BARON.   We've all seen better days—yes! I used to wake up in the morning and drink my coffee in bed—coffee—with cream! Yes—

LUKA.   And yet we're all human beings. Pretend all you want to, put on all the airs you wish, but man you were born, and man you must die. And as I watch I see that the wiser people get, the busier they get—and though from bad to worse, they still strive to improve—stubbornly—

THE BARON.   Who are you, old fellow? Where do you come from?

LUKA.   I?

THE BARON.   Are you a tramp?

LUKA.   We're all of us tramps—why—I've heard said that the very earth we walk on is nothing but a tramp in the universe.

THE BARON [*severely*].   Perhaps. But have you a passport?

LUKA [*after a short pause*].   And what are you—a police inspector?

PEPEL [*delighted*].   You scored, old fellow! Well, Barosha, you got it this time!

BUBNOFF.   Yes—our little aristocrat got his!

THE BARON [*embarrassed*].   What's the matter? I was only joking, old man. Why, brother, I haven't a passport, either.

BUBNOFF.   You lie!

THE BARON.   Oh—well—I have some sort of papers—but they have no value—

LUKA.   They're papers just the same—and no papers are any good—

PEPEL.   Baron—come on to the saloon with me—

THE BARON.   I'm ready. Good-bye, old man—you old scamp—

LUKA.   Maybe I am one, brother—

PEPEL [*near doorway*].   Come on—come on!

[*Leaves,* BARON *following him quickly.*]

LUKA.   Was he really once a Baron?

BUBNOFF.   Who knows? A gentleman—? Yes. That much he's even now. Occasionally it sticks out. He never got rid of the habit.

LUKA.   Nobility is like small-pox. A man may get over it—but it leaves marks . . .

BUBNOFF.   He's all right all the same—occasionally he kicks—as he did about your passport . . .

[ALYOSHKA *comes in, slightly drunk, with a concertina in his hand, whistling.*]

ALYOSHKA.   Hey there, lodgers!

BUBNOFF.   What are you yelling for?

ALYOSHKA.   Excuse me—I beg your pardon! I'm a well-bred man—

BUBNOFF.   On a spree again?

ALYOSHKA.   Right you are! A moment ago Medyakin, the precinct captain, threw me out of the police station and said: "Look here—I don't want as much as a smell of you to stay in the streets—d'you hear?" I'm a man of principles, and the boss croaks at me—and what's a boss anyway—pah!—it's all bosh—the boss is a drunkard. I don't make any demands on life. I want nothing—that's all. Offer me one ruble, offer me twenty—it doesn't affect me. [NASTYA *comes from the kitchen*] Offer me a million—I won't take it! And to think that I, a respectable man, should be ordered about by a pal of mine—and he a drunkard! I won't have it—I won't!

[NASTYA *stands in the doorway, shaking her head at* ALYOSHKA.]

LUKA [*good-naturedly*].   Well, boy, you're a bit confused—

BUBNOFF.   Aren't men fools!

ALYOSHKA [*stretches out on the floor*].   Here, eat me up alive—and I don't want anything. I'm a desperate man. Show me one better! Why am I worse than others? There! Medyakin said: "If you show yourself on the streets I smash your face!" And yet I shall go out—I'll go—and stretch out in the middle of the street—let them choke me—I don't want a thing!

NASTYA.   Poor fellow—only a boy—and he's already putting on such airs—

ALYOSHKA [*kneeling before her*].   Lady! Mademoiselle! *Parlez français*—? *Prix courrant?* I'm on a spree—

NASTYA [*in a loud whisper*].   Vassilisa!

VASSILISA [*opens door quickly; to* ALYOSHKA].   You here again?

ALYOSHKA.   How do you do—? Come in—you're welcome—

VASSILISA.   I told you, young puppy, that not a shadow of you should stick around here—and you're back—eh?

ALYOSHKA.   Vassilisa Karpovna . . . shall I tune up a funeral march for you?

VASSILISA [seizing him by the shoulders].   Get out!

ALYOSHKA [moving towards the door].   Wait—you can't put me out this way! I learned this funeral march a little while ago! It's refreshing music . . . wait—you can't put me out like that!

VASSILISA.   I'll show whether I can or not. I'll rouse the whole street against you—you foul-mouthed creature—you're too young to bark about me—

ALYOSHKA [running out].   All right—I'll go—

VASSILISA.   Look out—I'll get you yet!

ALYOSHKA [opens the door and shouts].   Vassilisa Karpovna—I'm not afraid of you—[Hides]

[LUKA laughs.]

VASSILISA.   Who are you?

LUKA.   A passer-by—a traveler . . .

VASSILISA.   Stopping for the night or going to stay here?

LUKA.   I'll see.

VASSILISA.   Have you a passport?

LUKA.   Yes.

VASSILISA.   Give it to me.

LUKA.   I'll bring it over to your house—

VASSILISA.   Call yourself a traveler? If you'd say a tramp—that would be nearer the truth—

LUKA [sighing].   You're not very kindly, mother!

[VASSILISA goes to door that leads to PEPEL's room, ALYOSHKA pokes his head through the kitchen door.]

ALYOSHKA.   Has she left?

VASSILISA [turning around].   Are you still here?

[ALYOSHKA disappears, whistling. NASTYA and LUKA laugh.]

BUBNOFF [to VASSILISA].   He isn't here—

VASSILISA.   Who?

BUBNOFF.   Vaska.

VASSILISA.   Did I ask you about him?

BUBNOFF.   I noticed you were looking around—

VASSILISA.   I am looking to see if things are in order, you see? Why aren't the floors swept yet? How often did I give orders to keep the house clean?

BUBNOFF.   It's the actor's turn to sweep—

VASSILISA.   Never mind whose turn it is! If the health inspector comes and fines me, I'll throw out the lot of you—

BUBNOFF [*calmly*].   Then how are you going to earn your living?

VASSILISA.   I don't want a speck of dirt! [*Goes to kitchen; to* NASTYA] What are you hanging round here for? Why's your face all swollen up? Why are you standing there like a dummy? Go on—sweep the floor! Did you see Natalia? Was she here?

NASTYA.   I don't know—I haven't seen her . . .

VASSILISA.   Bubnoff! Was my sister here?

BUBNOFF.   She brought him along.

VASSILISA.   That one—was he home?

BUBNOFF.   Vassily? Yes—Natalia was here talking to Kleshtch—

VASSILISA.   I'm not asking you whom she talked to. Dirt everywhere—filth—oh, you swine! Mop it all up—do you hear? [*Exits rapidly*]

BUBNOFF.   What a savage beast she is!

LUKA.   She's a lady that means business!

NASTYA.   You grow to be an animal, leading such a life—any human being tied to such a husband as hers . . .

BUBNOFF.   Well—that tie isn't worrying her any—

LUKA.   Does she always have these fits?

BUBNOFF.   Always. You see, she came to find her lover—but he isn't home—

LUKA.   I guess she was hurt. Oh-ho! Everybody is trying to be boss—and is threatening everybody else with all kinds of punishment—and still there's no order in life . . . and no cleanliness—

BUBNOFF.   All the world likes order—but some people's brains aren't fit for it. All the same—the room should be swept—Nastya—you ought to get busy!

NASTYA.   Oh, certainly! Anything else? Think I'm your servant? [*Silence*] I'm going to get drunk to-night—dead-drunk!

BUBNOFF.   Fine business!

LUKA.   Why do you want to get drunk, girlie? A while ago you were crying—and now you say you'll get drunk—

NASTYA [*defiantly*].   I'll drink—then I cry again—that's all there's to it!

BUBNOFF.   That's nothing!

LUKA.   But for what reason—tell me! Every pimple has a cause! [NASTYA *remains silent, shaking her head*] Oh—you men—what's to become of you? All right—I'll sweep the place. Where's your broom?

BUBNOFF.   Behind the door—in the hall—

[LUKA *goes into the hall.*]

Nastinka!

NASTYA.   Yes?

BUBNOFF.   Why did Vassilisa jump on Alyoshka?

NASTYA.   He told her that Vaska was tired of her and was going to get rid of her—and that he's going to make up to Natasha—I'll go away from here—I'll find another lodging-house—

BUBNOFF.   Why? Where?

NASTYA.   I'm sick of this—I'm not wanted here!

BUBNOFF [*calmly*].   You're not wanted anywhere—and, anyway, all people on earth are superfluous—

[NASTYA *shakes her head. Rises and slowly, quietly, leaves the cellar.*
MIEDVIEDIEFF *comes in.* LUKA, *with the broom, follows him.*]

MIEDVIEDIEFF.   I don't think I know you—

LUKA.   How about the others—d'you know them all?

MIEDVIEDIEFF.   I must know everybody in my precinct. But I don't know you.

LUKA.   That's because, uncle, the whole world can't stow itself away in your precinct—some of it was bound to remain outside . . . [*Goes into kitchen*]

MIEDVIEDIEFF [*crosses to* BUBNOFF].   It's true—my precinct is rather small—yet it's worse than any of the very largest. Just now, before getting off duty, I had to bring Alyoshka, the shoemaker, to the station house. Just imagine—there he was, stretched right in the middle of the street, playing his concertina and yelping: "I want nothing, nothing!" Horses going past all the time—and with all the traffic going on, he could easily have been run over—and so on! He's a wild youngster—so I just collared him—he likes to make mischief—

BUBNOFF.   Coming to play checkers to-night?

MIEDVIEDIEFF.   Yes—I'll come—how's Vaska?

BUBNOFF.   Same as ever—

MIEDVIEDIEFF.   Meaning—he's getting along—?

BUBNOFF.   Why shouldn't he? He's able to get along all right.

MIEDVIEDIEFF [*doubtfully*].   Why shouldn't he? [LUKA *goes into hallway, carrying a pail*] M-yes—there's a lot of talk about Vaska. Haven't you heard?

BUBNOFF.   I hear all sorts of gossip . . .

MIEDVIEDIEFF.   There seems to have been some sort of talk concerning Vassilisa. Haven't you heard about it?

BUBNOFF.   What?

MIEDVIEDIEFF. Oh—why—generally speaking. Perhaps you know—and lie. Everybody knows—[*Severely*] You mustn't lie, brother!

BUBNOFF. Why should I lie?

MIEDVIEDIEFF. That's right. Dogs! They say that Vaska and Vassilisa . . . but what's that to me? I'm not her father. I'm her uncle. Why should they ridicule me? [KVASHNYA *comes in*] What are people coming to? They laugh at everything. Aha—you here?

KVASHNYA. Well—my love-sick garrison—? Bubnoff! He came up to me again on the marketplace and started pestering me about marrying him . . .

BUBNOFF. Go to it! Why not? He has money and he's still a husky fellow.

MIEDVIEDIEFF. Me—? I should say so!

KVASHNYA. You ruffian! Don't you dare touch my sore spot! I've gone through it once already, darling. Marriage to a woman is just like jumping through a hole in the ice in winter. You do it once, and you remember it the rest of your life . . .

MIEDVIEDIEFF. Wait! There are different breeds of husbands . . .

KVASHNYA. But there's only one of me! When my beloved husband kicked the bucket, I spent the whole day all by my lonely—just bursting with joy. I sat and simply couldn't believe it was true. . . .

MIEDVIEDIEFF. If your husband beat you without cause, you should have complained to the police.

KVASHNYA. I complained to God for eight years—and he didn't help.

MIEDVIEDIEFF. Nowadays the law forbids to beat your wife . . . all is very strict these days—there's law and order everywhere. You can't beat up people without due cause. If you beat them to maintain discipline—all right . . .

LUKA [*comes in with* ANNA]. Well—we finally managed to get here after all. Oh, you! Why do you, weak as you are, walk about alone? Where's your bunk?

ANNA [*pointing*]. Thank you, grand-dad.

KVASHNYA. There—she's married—look at her!

LUKA. The little woman is in very bad shape . . . she was creeping along the hallway, clinging to the wall and moaning—why do you leave her by herself?

KVASHNYA. Oh, pure carelessness on our part, little father—forgive us! Her maid, it appears, went out for a walk . . .

LUKA. Go on—poke fun at me . . . but, all the same, how can you neglect a human being like that? No matter who or what, every human life has its worth . . .

MIEDVIEDIEFF. There should be supervision! Suppose she died

suddenly—? That would cause a lot of bother . . . we must look after her!

LUKA.   True, sergeant!

MIEDVIEDIEFF.   Well—yes—though I'm not a sergeant—ah—yet!

LUKA.   No! But you carry yourself most martially!

[*Noise of shuffling feet is heard in the hallway. Muffled cries.*]

MIEDVIEDIEFF.   What now—a row?

BUBNOFF.   Sounds like it?

KVASHNYA.   I'll go and see . . .

MIEDVIEDIEFF.   I'll go, too. It is my duty! Why separate people when they fight? They'll stop sooner or later of their own accord. One gets tired of fighting. Why not let them fight all they want to—freely? They wouldn't fight half as often—if they'd remember former beatings . . .

BUBNOFF [*climbing down from his bunk*].   Why don't you speak to your superiors about it?

KOSTILYOFF [*throws open the door and shouts*].   Abram! Come quick—Vassilisa is killing Natasha—come quick!

[KVASHNYA, MIEDVIEDIEFF, *and* BUBNOFF *rush into hallway;* LUKA *looks after them, shaking his head.*]

ANNA.   Oh God—poor little Natasha . . .

LUKA.   Who's fighting out there?

ANNA.   Our landladies—they're sisters . . .

LUKA [*crossing to* ANNA].   Why?

ANNA.   Oh—for no reason—except that they're both fat and healthy . . .

LUKA.   What's your name?

ANNA.   Anna . . . I look at you . . . you're like my father—my dear father . . . you're as gentle as he was—and as soft. . . .

LUKA.   Soft! Yes! They pounded me till I got soft! [*Laughs tremulously*]

CURTAIN

Act II

Same as Act I — Night.

On the bunks near the stove SATINE, THE BARON, KRIVOY ZOB, *and* THE
  TARTAR *play cards.* KLESHTCH *and* THE ACTOR *watch them.*
  BUBNOFF, *on his bunk, is playing checkers with* MIEDVIEDIEFF.
  LUKA *sits on a stool by* ANNA's *bedside. The place is lit by two
  lamps, one on the wall near the card players, the other is on*
  BUBNOFF's *bunk.*

THE TARTAR. I'll play one more game — then I'll stop . . .
BUBNOFF. Zob! Sing! [*He sings*]

> "The sun rises and sets . . ."

ZOB [*joining in*].

> "But my prison is dark, dark . . ."

THE TARTAR [*to* SATINE]. Shuffle the cards — and shuffle them
well. We know your kind —
ZOB AND BUBNOFF [*together*].

> "Day and night the wardens
> Watch beneath my window . . ."

ANNA. Blows — insults — I've had nothing but that all my life
long . . .
LUKA. Don't worry, little mother!
MIEDVIEDIEFF. Look where you're moving!
BUBNOFF. Oh, yes — that's right . . .
THE TARTAR [*threatening* SATINE *with his fist*]. You're trying to
palm a card? I've seen you — you scoundrel . . .

21

ZOB.   Stop it, Hassan! They'll skin us anyway . . . come in, Bubnoff!

ANNA.   I can't remember a single day when I didn't go hungry . . . I've been afraid, waking, eating, and sleeping . . . all my life I've trembled—afraid I wouldn't get another bite . . . all my life I've been in rags—all through my wretched life—and why . . . ?

LUKA.   Yes, yes, child—you're tired—never you mind!

THE ACTOR [*to* ZOB].   Play the Jack—the Jack, devil take you!

THE BARON.   And we play the King!

KLESHTCH.   They always win.

SATINE.   Such is our habit.

MIEDVIEDIEFF.   I have the Queen!

BUBNOFF.   And so have I!

ANNA.   I'm dying . . .

KLESHTCH.   Look, look! Prince, throw up the game—throw it up, I tell you!

THE ACTOR.   Can't he play without your assistance?

THE BARON.   Look out, Andrushka, or I'll beat the life out of you!

THE TARTAR.   Deal once more—the pitcher went after water—and got broke—and so did I!

[KLESHTCH *shakes his head and crosses to* BUBNOFF.]

ANNA.   I keep on thinking—is it possible that I'll suffer in the other world as I did in this—is it possible? There, too?

LUKA.   Nothing of the sort! Don't you disturb yourself! You'll rest there . . . be patient. We all suffer, dear, each in our own way. . . . [*Rises and goes quickly into kitchen*]

BUBNOFF [*sings*].

"Watch as long as you please . . ."

ZOB.   "I shan't run away . . ."

BOTH [*together*].

"I long to be free, free—
    Alas! I cannot break my chains. . . ."

THE TARTAR [*yells*].   That card was up his sleeve!

THE BARON [*embarrassed*].   Do you want me to shove it up your nose?

THE ACTOR [*emphatically*].   Prince! You're mistaken—nobody—ever . . .

THE TARTAR.   I saw it! You cheat! I won't play!

SATINE [*gathering up the cards*].   Leave us alone, Hassan . . . you knew right along that we're cheats—why did you play with us?

THE BARON.   He lost forty kopecks and he yelps as if he had lost a fortune! And a Prince at that!

THE TARTAR [*excitedly*].   Then play honest!

SATINE.   What for?

THE TARTAR.   What do you mean "what for"?

SATINE.   Exactly. What for?

THE TARTAR.   Don't you know?

SATINE.   I don't. Do you?

[THE TARTAR *spits out, furiously; the others laugh at him.*]

ZOB [*good-naturedly*].   You're a funny fellow, Hassan! Try to understand this! If they should begin to live honestly, they'd die of starvation inside of three days.

THE TARTAR.   That's none of my business. You must live honestly!

ZOB.   They did you brown! Come and let's have tea. . . . [*Sings*]

"O my chains, my heavy chains . . ."

BUBNOFF [*sings*].

"You're my steely, clanking wardens . . ."

ZOB.   Come on, Hassanka! [*Leaves the room, singing*]

"I cannot tear you, cannot break you . . ."

[THE TARTAR *shakes his fist threateningly at* THE BARON, *and follows the other out of the room.*]

SATINE [*to* BARON, *laughing*].   Well, Your Imperial Highness, you've again sat down magnificently in a mud puddle! You've learned a lot—but you're an ignoramus when it comes to palming a card.

THE BARON [*spreading his hands*].   The devil knows how it happened. . . .

THE ACTOR.   You're not gifted—you've no faith in yourself—and without that you can never accomplish anything . . .

MIEDVIEDIEFF.   I've one Queen—and you've two—oh, well . . .

BUBNOFF.   One's enough if she has brains—play!

KLESHTCH.   You lost, Abram Ivanovitch?

MIEDVIEDIEFF.   None of your business—see? Shut up!

SATINE.   I've won fifty-three kopecks.

THE ACTOR.   Give me three of them . . . though, what'll I do with them?

LUKA [*coming from kitchen*].   Well—the Tartar was fleeced all right, eh? Going to have some vodka?

THE BARON.   Come with us.

SATINE.   I wonder what you'll be like when you're drunk.

LUKA.   Same as when I'm sober.

THE ACTOR.   Come on, old man—I'll recite verses for you . . .

LUKA.   What?

THE ACTOR.   Verses. Don't you understand?

LUKA.   Verses? And what do I want with verses?

THE ACTOR.   Sometimes they're funny—sometimes sad.

SATINE.   Well, poet, are you coming? [*Exits with* THE BARON]

THE ACTOR.   I'm coming. I'll join you. For instance, old man, here's a bit of verse—I forget how it begins—I forget . . . [*brushes his hand across his forehead*]

BUBNOFF.   There! Your Queen is lost—go on, play!

MIEDVIEDIEFF.   I made the wrong move.

THE ACTOR.   Formerly, before my organism was poisoned with alcohol, old man, I had a good memory. But now it's all over with me, brother. I used to declaim these verses with tremendous success— thunders of applause . . . you have no idea what applause means . . . it goes to your head like vodka! I'd step out on the stage—stand this way—[*Strikes a pose*]—I'd stand there and . . . [*Pause*] I can't remember a word—I can't remember! My favorite verses—isn't it ghastly, old man?

LUKA.   Yes—is there anything worse than forgetting what you loved? Your very soul is in the thing you love!

THE ACTOR.   I've drunk my soul away, old man—brother, I'm lost . . . and why? Because I had no faith. . . . I'm done with . . .

LUKA.   Well—then—cure yourself! Nowadays they have a cure for drunkards. They treat you free of charge, brother. There's a hospital for drunkards—where they're treated for nothing. They've owned up, you see, that even a drunkard is a human being, and they're only too glad to help him get well. Well—then—go to it!

THE ACTOR [*thoughtfully*].   Where? Where is it?

LUKA.   Oh—in some town or other . . . what do they call it—? I'll tell you the name presently—only, in the meanwhile, get ready. Don't drink so much! Take yourself in hand—and bear up! And then, when you're cured, you'll begin life all over again. Sounds good, brother, doesn't it, to begin all over again? Well—make up your mind!

THE ACTOR [*smiling*].   All over again—from the very beginning— that's fine . . . yes . . . all over again . . . [*Laughs*] Well—then—I can, can't I?

LUKA.   Why not? A human being can do anything—if he only makes up his mind.

THE ACTOR [*suddenly, as if coming out of a trance*].   You're a queer bird! See you anon! [*Whistles*] Old man—*au revoir!* [*Exits*]

ANNA. Grand-dad!
LUKA. Yes, little mother?
ANNA. Talk to me.
LUKA [*close to her*]. Come on—let's chat . . .

[KLESHTCH, *glancing around, silently walks over to his wife, looks at her, and makes queer gestures with his hands, as though he wanted to say something.*]

LUKA: What is it, brother?
KLESHTCH [*quietly*]. Nothing . . .

[*Crosses slowly to hallway door, stands on the threshold for a few seconds, and exits.*]

LUKA [*looking after him*]. Hard on your man, isn't it?
ANNA. He doesn't concern me much . . .
LUKA. Did he beat you?
ANNA. Worse than that—it's he who's killed me—
BUBNOFF. My wife used to have a lover—the scoundrel—how clever he was at checkers!
MIEDVIEDIEFF. Hm-hm—
ANNA. Grand-dad! Talk to me, darling—I feel so sick . . .
LUKA. Never mind—it's always like this before you die, little dove—never mind, dear! Just have faith! Once you're dead, you'll have peace—always. There's nothing to be afraid of—nothing. Quiet! Peace! Lie quietly! Death wipes out everything. Death is kindly. You die—and you rest—that's what they say. It is true, dear! Because—where can we find rest on this earth?

[PEPEL *enters. He is slightly drunk, disheveled, and sullen. Sits down on bunk near door, and remains silent and motionless.*]

ANNA. And how is it—there? More suffering?
LUKA. Nothing of the kind! No suffering! Trust me! Rest—nothing else! They'll lead you into God's presence, and they'll say: "Dear God! Behold! Here is Anna, Thy servant!"
MIEDVIEDIEFF [*sternly*]. How do you know what they'll say up there? Oh, you . . .

[PEPEL, *on hearing* MIEDVIEDIEFF'*s voice, raises his head and listens.*]

LUKA. Apparently I do know, Mr. Sergeant!
MIEDVIEDIEFF [*conciliatory*]. Yes—it's your own affair—though I'm not exactly a sergeant—yet—
BUBNOFF. I jump two!

MIEDVIEDIEFF. Damn—play!

LUKA. And the Lord will look at you gently and tenderly and He'll say: "I know this Anna!" Then He'll say: "Take Anna into Paradise. Let her have peace. I know. Her life on earth was hard. She is very weary. Let Anna rest in peace!"

ANNA [*choking*]. Grandfather—if it were only so—if there were only rest and peace . . .

LUKA. There won't be anything else! Trust me! Die in joy and not in grief. Death is to us like a mother to small children . . .

ANNA. But—perhaps—perhaps I'll get well . . . ?

LUKA [*laughing*]. Why—? Just to suffer more?

ANNA. But—just to live a little longer . . . just a little longer! Since there'll be no suffering hereafter, I could bear it a little longer down here . . .

LUKA. There'll be nothing in the hereafter . . . but only . . .

PEPEL [*rising*]. Maybe yes—maybe no!

ANNA [*frightened*]. Oh—God!

LUKA. Hey—Adonis!

MIEDVIEDIEFF. Who's that yelping?

PEPEL [*crossing over to him*]. I! What of it?

MIEDVIEDIEFF. You yelp needlessly—that's what! People ought to have some dignity!

PEPEL. Block-head! And that's an uncle for you—ho-ho!

LUKA [*to* PEPEL, *in an undertone*]. Look here—don't shout—this woman's dying—her lips are already grey—don't disturb her!

PEPEL. I've respect for you, grand-dad. You're all right, you are! You lie well, and you spin pleasant yarns. Go on lying, brother—there's little fun in this world . . .

BUBNOFF. Is the woman really dying?

LUKA. You think I'm joking?

BUBNOFF. That means she'll stop coughing. Her cough was very disturbing. I jump two!

MIEDVIEDIEFF. I'd like to murder you!

PEPEL. Abramka!

MIEDVIEDIEFF. I'm not Abramka to you!

PEPEL. Abrashka! Is Natasha ill?

MIEDVIEDIEFF. None of your business!

PEPEL. Come—tell me! Did Vassilisa beat her up very badly?

MIEDVIEDIEFF. That's none of your business, either! It's a family affair! Who are you anyway?

PEPEL. Whoever I am, you'll never see Natashka again if I choose!

MIEDVIEDIEFF [*throwing up the game*]. What's that? Who are you alluding to? My niece by any chance? You thief!

PEPEL.   A thief whom you were never able to catch!

MIEDVIEDIEFF.   Wait—I'll catch you yet—you'll see—sooner than you think!

PEPEL.   If you catch me, God help your whole nest! Do you think I'll keep quiet before the examining magistrate? Every wolf howls! They'll ask me: "Who made you steal and showed you where?" "Mishka Kostilyoff and his wife!" "Who was your fence?" "Mishka Kostilyoff and his wife!"

MIEDVIEDIEFF.   You lie! No one will believe you!

PEPEL.   They'll believe me all right—because it's the truth! And I'll drag you into it, too. Ha! I'll ruin the lot of you—devils—just watch!

MIEDVIEDIEFF [*confused*].   You lie! You lie! And what harm did I do to you, you mad dog?

PEPEL.   And what good did you ever do me?

LUKA.   That's right!

MIEDVIEDIEFF [*to* LUKA].   Well—what are you croaking about? Is it any of your business? This is a family matter!

BUBNOFF [*to* LUKA].   Leave them alone! What do we care if they twist each other's tails?

LUKA [*peacefully*].   I meant no harm. All I said was that if a man isn't good to you, then he's acting wrong . . .

MIEDVIEDIEFF [*uncomprehending*].   Now then—we all of us here know each other—but you—who are you? [*Frowns and exits*]

LUKA.   The cavalier is peeved! Oh-ho, brothers, I see your affairs are a bit tangled up!

PEPEL.   He'll run to complain about us to Vassilisa . . .

BUBNOFF.   You're a fool, Vassily. You're very bold these days, aren't you? Watch out! It's all right to be bold when you go gathering mushrooms, but what good is it here? They'll break your neck before you know it!

PEPEL.   Well—not as fast as all that! You don't catch us Yaroslavl boys napping! If it's going to be war, we'll fight . . .

LUKA.   Look here, boy, you really ought to go away from here—

PEPEL.   Where? Please tell me!

LUKA.   Go to Siberia!

PEPEL.   If I go to Siberia, it'll be at the Tsar's expense!

LUKA.   Listen! You go just the same! You can make your own way there. They need your kind out there . . .

PEPEL.   My way is clear. My father spent all his life in prison, and I inherited the trait. Even when I was a small child, they called me thief—thief's son.

LUKA.   But Siberia is a fine country—a land of gold. Any one who has health and strength and brains can live there like a cucumber in a hot-house.

PEPEL.   Old man, why do you always tell lies?

LUKA.   What?

PEPEL.   Are you deaf? I ask—why do you always lie?

LUKA.   What do I lie about?

PEPEL.   About everything. According to you, life's wonderful everywhere—but you lie . . . why?

LUKA.   Try to believe me. Go and see for yourself. And some day you'll thank me for it. What are you hanging round here for? And, besides, why is truth so important to you? Just think! Truth may spell death to you!

PEPEL.   It's all one to me! If that—let it be that!

LUKA.   Oh—what a madman! Why should you kill yourself?

BUBNOFF.   What are you two jawing about, anyway? I don't understand. What kind of truth do you want, Vaska? And what for? You know the truth about yourself—and so does everybody else . . .

PEPEL.   Just a moment! Don't crow! Let him tell me! Listen, old man! Is there a God?

[LUKA *smiles silently.*]

BUBNOFF.   People just drift along—like shavings on a stream. When a house is built—the shavings are thrown away!

PEPEL.   Well? Is there a God? Tell me.

LUKA [*in a low voice*].   If you have faith, there is; if you haven't, there isn't . . . whatever you believe in, exists . . .

[PEPEL *looks at* LUKA *in staring surprise.*]

BUBNOFF.   I'm going to have tea—come on over to the restaurant!

LUKA [*to* PEPEL].   What are you staring at?

PEPEL.   Oh—just because! Wait now—you mean to say . . .

BUBNOFF.   Well—I'm off.

[*Goes to door and runs into* VASSILISA.]

PEPEL.   So—you . . .

VASSILISA [*to* BUBNOFF].   Is Nastasya home?

BUBNOFF.   No. [*Exits*]

PEPEL.   Oh—you've come—?

VASSILISA [*crossing to* ANNA].   Is she alive yet?

LUKA.   Don't disturb her!

VASSILISA.   What are you loafing around here for?

LUKA.   I'll go—if you want me to . . .

VASSILISA [*turning toward* PEPEL'*s room*].   Vassily! I've some business with you . . .

[LUKA *goes to hallway door, opens it, and shuts it loudly, then warily climbs into a bunk, and from there to the top of the stove.*]

VASSILISA [*calling from* PEPEL'*s room*].   Vaska—come here!
PEPEL.   I won't come—I don't want to . . .
VASSILISA.   Why? What are you angry about?
PEPEL.   I'm sick of the whole thing . . .
VASSILISA.   Sick of me, too?
PEPEL.   Yes! Of you, too!

[VASSILISA *draws her shawl about her, pressing her hands over her breast. Crosses to* ANNA, *looks carefully through the bed curtains, and returns to* PEPEL.]

Well—out with it!
VASSILISA.   What do you want me to say? I can't force you to be loving, and I'm not the sort to beg for kindness. Thank you for telling me the truth.
PEPEL.   What truth?
VASSILISA.   That you're sick of me—or isn't it the truth? [PEPEL *looks at her silently. She turns to him*] What are you staring at? Don't you recognize me?
PEPEL [*sighing*].   You're beautiful, Vassilisa! [*She puts her arm about his neck, but he shakes it off*] But I never gave my heart to you. . . . I've lived with you and all that—but I never really liked you . . .
VASSILISA [*quietly*].   That so? Well—?
PEPEL.   What is there to talk about? Nothing. Go away from me!
VASSILISA.   Taken a fancy to some one else?
PEPEL.   None of your business! Suppose I have—I wouldn't ask you to be my match-maker!
VASSILISA [*significantly*].   That's too bad . . . perhaps I might arrange a match . . .
PEPEL [*suspiciously*].   Who with?
VASSILISA.   You know—why do you pretend? Vassily—let me be frank. [*With lower voice*] I won't deny it—you've offended me . . . it was like a bolt from the blue . . . you said you loved me—and then all of a sudden . . .
PEPEL.   It wasn't sudden at all. It's been a long time since I . . . woman, you've no soul! A woman must have a soul . . . we men are beasts—we must be taught—and you, what have you taught me—?
VASSILISA.   Never mind the past! I know—no man owns his own

heart—you don't love me any longer . . . well and good, it can't be helped!

PEPEL.   So that's over. We part peaceably, without a row—as it should be!

VASSILISA.   Just a moment! All the same, when I lived with you, I hoped you'd help me out of this swamp—I thought you'd free me from my husband and my uncle—from all this life—and perhaps, Vassya, it wasn't you whom I loved—but my hope—do you understand? I waited for you to drag me out of this mire . . .

PEPEL.   You aren't a nail—and I'm not a pair of pincers! I thought you had brains—you are so clever—so crafty . . .

VASSILISA [*leaning closely toward him*].   Vassa—let's help each other!

PEPEL.   How?

VASSILISA [*low and forcibly*].   My sister—I know you've fallen for her . . .

PEPEL.   And that's why you beat her up, like the beast you are! Look out, Vassilisa! Don't you touch her!

VASSILISA.   Wait. Don't get excited. We can do everything quietly and pleasantly. You want to marry her. I'll give you money . . . three hundred rubles—even more than that . . .

PEPEL [*moving away from her*].   Stop! What do you mean?

VASSILISA.   Rid me of my husband! Take that noose from around my neck . . .

PEPEL [*whistling softly*].   So that's the way the land lies! You certainly planned it cleverly . . . in other words, the grave for the husband, the gallows for the lover, and as for yourself . . .

VASSILISA.   Vassya! Why the gallows? It doesn't have to be yourself—but one of your pals! And supposing it were yourself—who'd know? Natalia—just think—and you'll have money—you go away somewhere—you free me forever—and it'll be very good for my sister to be away from me—the sight of her enrages me. . . . I get furious with her on account of you, and I can't control myself. I tortured the girl— I beat her up—beat her up so that I myself cried with pity for her—but I'll beat her—and I'll go on beating her!

PEPEL.   Beast! Bragging about your beastliness?

VASSILISA.   I'm not bragging—I speak the truth. Think now, Vassa. You've been to prison twice because of my husband—through his greed. He clings to me like a bed-bug—he's been sucking the life out of me for the last four years—and what sort of a husband is he to me? He's forever abusing Natasha—calls her a beggar—he's just poison, plain poison, to every one . . .

PEPEL.   You spin your yarn cleverly . . .

VASSILISA.   Everything I say is true. Only a fool could be as blind as you . . .

[KOSTILYOFF *enters stealthily and comes forward noisily.*]

PEPEL [*to* VASSILISA].   Oh—go away!

VASSILISA.   Think it over! [*Sees her husband*] What? You? Following me?

[PEPEL *leaps up and stares at* KOSTILYOFF *savagely.*]

KOSTILYOFF.   It's I, I! So the two of you were here alone—you were—ah—conversing? [*Suddenly stamps his feet and screams*] Vassilisa—you bitch! You beggar! You damned hag! [*Frightened by his own screams, which are met by silence and indifference on the part of the others*] Forgive me, O Lord . . . Vassilisa—again you've led me into the path of sin. . . . I've been looking for you everywhere. It's time to go to bed. You forgot to fill the lamps—oh, you . . . beggar! Swine! [*Shakes his trembling fist at her, while* VASSILISA *slowly goes to door, glancing at* PEPEL *over her shoulder*]

PEPEL [*to* KOSTILYOFF].   Go away—clear out of here—

KOSTILYOFF [*yelling*].   What? I? The Boss? I get out? You thief!

PEPEL [*sullenly*].   Go away, Mishka!

KOSTILYOFF.   Don't you dare—I—I'll show you.

[PEPEL *seizes him by the collar and shakes him. From the stove come loud noises and yawns.* PEPEL *releases* KOSTILYOFF *who runs into the hallway, screaming.*]

PEPEL [*jumping on a bunk*].   Who is it? Who's on the stove?

LUKA [*raising his head*].   Eh?

PEPEL.   You?

LUKA [*undisturbed*].   I—I myself—oh, dear Jesus!

PEPEL [*shuts hallway door, looks for the wooden closing bar, but can't find it*].   The devil! Come down, old man!

LUKA.   I'm climbing down—all right . . .

PEPEL [*roughly*].   What did you climb on that stove for?

LUKA.   Where was I to go?

PEPEL.   Why—didn't you go out into the hall?

LUKA.   The hall's too cold for an old fellow like myself, brother.

PEPEL.   You overheard?

LUKA.   Yes—I did. How could I help it? Am I deaf? Well, my boy, happiness is coming your way. Real, good fortune I call it!

PEPEL [*suspiciously*].   What good fortune—?

LUKA.   In so far as I was lying on the stove . . .

PEPEL.   Why did you make all that noise?

LUKA.   Because I was getting warm . . . it was your good luck . . . I thought if only the boy wouldn't make a mistake and choke the old man . . .

PEPEL.   Yes—I might have done it . . . how terrible . . .

LUKA.   Small wonder! It isn't difficult to make a mistake of that sort.

PEPEL [*smiling*].   What's the matter? Did you make the same sort of mistake once upon a time?

LUKA.   Boy, listen to me. Send that woman out of your life! Don't let her near you! Her husband—she'll get rid of him herself—and in a shrewder way than you could—yes! Don't you listen to that devil! Look at me! I am bald-headed—know why? Because of all these women. . . . Perhaps I knew more women than I had hair on the top of my head— but this Vassilisa—she's worse than the plague . . .

PEPEL.   I don't understand . . . I don't know whether to thank you— or—well . . .

LUKA.   Don't say a word! You won't improve on what I said. Listen: take the one you like by the arm, and march out of here—get out of here—clean out . . .

PEPEL [*sadly*].   I can't understand people. Who is kind and who isn't? It's all a mystery to me . . .

LUKA.   What's there to understand? There's all breeds of men . . . they all live as their hearts tell them . . . good to-day, bad to-morrow! But if you really care for that girl . . . take her away from here and that's all there is to it. Otherwise go away alone . . . you're young—you're in no hurry for a wife . . .

PEPEL [*taking him by the shoulder*].   Tell me! Why do you say all this?

LUKA.   Wait. Let me go. I want to look at Anna . . . she was coughing so terribly . . . [*Goes to* ANNA's *bed, pulls the curtains, looks, touches her.* PEPEL *thoughtfully and distraught, follows him with his eyes*] Merciful Jesus Christ! Take into Thy keeping the soul of this woman Anna, new-comer amongst the blessed!

PEPEL [*softly*].   Is she dead?

[*Without approaching, he stretches himself and looks at the bed.*]

LUKA [*gently*].   Her sufferings are over! Where's her husband?

PEPEL.   In the saloon, most likely . . .

LUKA.   Well—he'll have to be told . . .

PEPEL [*shuddering*].   I don't like corpses!

LUKA [*going to door*].   Why should you like them? It's the living who demand our love—the living . . .

PEPEL.   I'm coming with you . . .

LUKA.   Are you afraid?

PEPEL.   I don't like it . . .

[*They go out quickly. The stage is empty and silent for a few mo-
ments. Behind the door is heard a dull, staccato, incomprehensi-
ble noise. Then* THE ACTOR *enters.*]

THE ACTOR [*stands at the open door, supporting himself against the
jamb, and shouts*].   Hey, old man—where are you—? I just remem-
bered—listen . . . [*Takes two staggering steps forward and, striking a
pose, recites*]

> "Good people! If the world cannot find
> A path to holy truth,
> Glory be to the madman who will enfold all humanity
> In a golden dream . . ."

[NATASHA *appears in the doorway behind* THE ACTOR.]

Old man! [*recites*]

> "If to-morrow the sun were to forget
> To light our earth,
> To-morrow then some madman's thought
> Would bathe the world in sunshine. . . ."

NATASHA [*laughing*].   Scarecrow! You're drunk!

THE ACTOR [*turns to her*].   Oh—it's you! Where's the old man, the
dear old man? Not a soul here, seems to me . . . Natasha, farewell—
right—farewell!

NATASHA [*entering*].   Don't wish me farewell, before you've wished
me how-d'you-do!

THE ACTOR [*barring her way*].   I am going. Spring will come—and
I'll be here no longer—

NATASHA.   Wait a moment! Where do you propose going?

THE ACTOR.   In search of a town—to be cured—And you, Ophelia,
must go away! Take the veil! Just imagine—there's a hospital to cure—
ah—organisms for drunkards—a wonderful hospital—built of marble—with marble floors . . . light—clean—food—and all gratis! And a
marble floor—yes! I'll find it—I'll get cured—and then I shall start life
anew. . . . I'm on my way to regeneration, as King Lear said. Natasha,
my stage name is . . . Svertchkoff—Zavoloushski . . . do you realize how
painful it is to lose one's name? Even dogs have their names . . .

[NATASHA *carefully passes* THE ACTOR, *stops at* ANNA's *bed and
looks.*]

To be nameless—is not to exist!

NATASHA.   Look, my dear—why—she's dead. . . .

THE ACTOR [*shakes his head*].   Impossible . . .

NATASHA [*stepping back*].   So help me God—look . . .

BUBNOFF [*appearing in doorway*].   What is there to look at?

NATASHA.   Anna—she's dead!

BUBNOFF.   That means—she's stopped coughing! [*Goes to* ANNA's *bed, looks, and returns to his bunk*] We must tell Kleshtch—it's his business to know . . .

THE ACTOR.   I'll go—I'll say to him—she lost her name—[*Exits*]

NATASHA [*in centre of room*].   I, too—some day—I'll be found in the cellar—dead. . . .

BUBNOFF [*spreading out some rags on his bunk*].   What's that? What are you muttering?

NATASHA.   Nothing much . . .

BUBNOFF.   Waiting for Vaska, eh? Take care—Vassilisa'll break your head!

NATASHA.   Isn't it the same who breaks it? I'd much rather he'd do it!

BUBNOFF [*lying down*].   Well—that's your own affair . . .

NATASHA.   It's best for her to be dead—yet it's a pity . . . oh, Lord—why do we live?

BUBNOFF.   It's so with all . . . we're born, live, and die—and I'll die, too—and so'll you—what's there to be gloomy about?

[*Enter* LUKA, THE TARTAR, ZOB, *and* KLESHTCH. *The latter comes after the others, slowly, shrunk up.*]

NATASHA.   Sh-sh! Anna!

ZOB.   We've heard—God rest her soul . . .

THE TARTAR [*to* KLESHTCH].   We must take her out of here. Out into the hall! This is no place for corpses—but for the living . . .

KLESHTCH [*quietly*].   We'll take her out—

[*Everybody goes to the bed,* KLESHTCH *looks at his wife over the others' shoulders.*]

ZOB [*to* THE TARTAR].   You think she'll smell? I don't think she will—she dried up while she was still alive . . .

NATASHA.   God! If they'd only a little pity . . . if only some one would say a kindly word—oh, you . . .

LUKA.   Don't be hurt, girl—never mind! Why and how should we pity the dead? Come, dear! We don't pity the living—we can't even pity our own selves—how can we?

BUBNOFF [*yawning*].   And, besides, when you're dead, no word will help you—when you're still alive, even sick, it may. . . .

THE TARTAR [*stepping aside*].   The police must be notified . . .

ZOB.   The police—must be done! Kleshtch! Did you notify the police?

KLESHTCH.   No—she's got to be buried—and all I have is forty
kopecks—

ZOB.   Well—you'll have to borrow then—otherwise we'll take up a
collection—one'll give five kopecks, others as much as they can. But
the police must be notified at once—or they'll think you killed her or
God knows what not . . .

[*Crosses to* THE TARTAR's *bunk and prepares to lie down by his side.*]

NATASHA [*going to* BUBNOFF's *bunk*].   Now—I'll dream of her . . . I
always dream of the dead . . . I'm afraid to go out into the hall by myself—it's dark there . . .

LUKA [*following her*].   You better fear the living—I'm telling you . . .

NATASHA.   Take me across the hall, grandfather.

LUKA.   Come on—come on—I'll take you across—

[*They go away. Pause.*]

ZOB [*to* THE TARTAR].   Oh-ho! Spring will soon be here, little
brother, and it'll be quite warm. In the villages the peasants are already
making ready their ploughs and harrows, preparing to till . . . and we
. . . Hassan? Snoring already? Damned Mohammedan!

BUBNOFF.   Tartars love sleep!

KLESHTCH [*in centre of room, staring in front of him*].   What am I to
do now?

ZOB.   Lie down and sleep—that's all . . .

KLESHTCH [*softly*].   But—she . . . how about . . .

[*No one answers him.* SATINE *and* THE ACTOR *enter.*]

THE ACTOR [*yelling*].   Old man! Come here, my trusted Duke of
Kent!

SATINE.   Miklookha-Maklai is coming—ho-ho!

THE ACTOR.   It has been decided upon! Old man, where's the
town—where are you?

SATINE.   Fata Morgana, the old man bilked you from top to bottom!
There's nothing—no towns—no people—nothing at all!

THE ACTOR.   You lie!

THE TARTAR [*jumping up*].   Where's the boss? I'm going to the boss.
If I can't sleep, I won't pay! Corpses—drunkards . . .[*Exits quickly*]

[SATINE *looks after him and whistles.*]

BUBNOFF [*in a sleepy voice*].   Go to bed, boys—be quiet . . . night is
for sleep . . .

THE ACTOR. Yes—so—there's a corpse here. . . . "Our net fished up a corpse. . . ." Verses—by Béranger. . . .

SATINE [*screams*]. The dead can't hear . . . the dead do not feel— Scream!—Roar! . . . the deaf don't hear!

[*In the doorway appears* LUKA.]

CURTAIN

Act III

"The Waste," a yard strewn with rubbish and overgrown with weeds. Back, a high brick wall which shuts out the sight of the sky. Near it are elder bushes. Right, the dark, wooden wall of some sort of house, barn or stable. Left, the grey, tumbledown wall of KOSTILYOFF's *night asylum. It is built at an angle so that the further corner reaches almost to the centre of the yard. Between it and the wall runs a narrow passage. In the grey, plastered wall are two windows, one on a level with the ground, the other about six feet higher up and closer to the brick wall. Near the latter wall is a big sledge turned upside down and a beam about twelve feet long. Right of the wall is a heap of old planks. Evening. The sun is setting, throwing a crimson light on the brick wall. Early spring, the snow having only recently melted. The elder bushes are not yet in bud.*

NATASHA *and* NASTYA *are sitting side by side on the beam.* LUKA *and* THE BARON *are on the sledge.* KLESHTCH *is stretched on the pile of planks to the right.* BUBNOFF's *face is at the ground floor window.*

NASTYA [*with closed eyes, nodding her head in rhythm to the tale she is telling in a sing-song voice*].   So then at night he came into the garden. I had been waiting for him quite a while. I trembled with fear and grief—he trembled, too . . . he was as white as chalk—and he had the pistol in his hand . . .

NATASHA [*chewing sun-flower seeds*].   Oh—are these students really such desperate fellows . . . ?

NASTYA.   And he says to me in a dreadful voice: "My precious darling . . ."

BUBNOFF.   Ho-ho! Precious—?

37

THE BARON.   Shut up! If you don't like it, you can lump it! But
don't interrupt her. . . . Go on . . .

NASTYA.   "My one and only love," he says, "my parents," he says,
"refuse to give their consent to our wedding—and threaten to disown
me because of my love for you. Therefore," he says, "I must take my
life." And his pistol was huge—and loaded with ten bullets . . .
"Farewell," he says, "beloved comrade! I have made up my mind for
good and all . . . I can't live without you . . ." and I replied: "My unfor-
gettable friend—my Raoul. . . ."

BUBNOFF [surprised].   What? What? Krawl—did you call him—?

THE BARON.   Nastka! But last time his name was Gaston. . . .

NASTYA [jumping up].   Shut up, you bastards! Ah—you lousy mon-
grels! You think for a moment that you can understand love—true
love? My love was real honest-to-God love! [To THE BARON] You good-
for-nothing! . . . educated, you call yourself—drinking coffee in bed,
did you?

LUKA.   Now, now! Wait, people! Don't interfere! Show a little respect to your neighbors . . . it isn't the word that matters, but what's in
back of the word. That's what matters! Go on, girl! It's all right!

BUBNOFF.   Go on, crow! See if you can make your feathers white!

THE BARON.   Well—continue!

NATASHA.   Pay no attention to them . . . what are they? They're just
jealous . . . they've nothing to tell about themselves . . .

NASTYA [sits down again].   I'm going to say no more! If they don't
believe me they'll laugh. [Stops suddenly, is silent for a few seconds,
then, shutting her eyes, continues in a loud and intense voice, swaying
her hands as if to the rhythm of far music] And then I replied to him:
"Joy of my life! My bright moon! And I, too, I can't live without you—
because I love you madly, so madly—and I shall keep on loving you as
long as my heart beats in my bosom. But—" I say—"don't take your
young life! Think how necessary it is to your dear parents whose only
happiness you are. Leave me! Better that I should perish from longing
for you, my life! I alone! I—ah—as such, such! Better that I should
die—it doesn't matter . . . I am of no use to the world—and I have
nothing, nothing at all—" [Covers her face with her hand and weeps
gently]

NATASHA [in a low voice].   Don't cry—don't!

[LUKA, smiling, strokes NASTYA's head.]

BUBNOFF [laughs].   Ah—you limb of Satan!

THE BARON [also laughs].   Hey, old man? Do you think it's true? It's
all from that book "Fatal Love" . . . it's all nonsense! Let her alone!

NATASHA.   And what's it to you? Shut up—or God'll punish you!

NASTYA [*bitterly*].   God damn your soul! You worthless pig! Soul—
bah!—you haven't got one!

LUKA [*takes* NASTYA's *hand*].   Come, dear! It's nothing! Don't be
angry—I know—I believe you! You're right, not they! If you believe you
had a real love affair, then you did—yes! And as for him—don't be
angry with a fellow-lodger . . . maybe he's really jealous, and that's why
he's laughing. Maybe he never had any real love—maybe not—come
on—let's go!

NASTYA [*pressing her hand against her breast*].   Grandfather! So
help me God—it happened! It happened! He was a student, a
Frenchman—Gastotcha was his name—he had a little black beard—
and patent leathers—may God strike me dead if I'm lying! And he
loved me so—my God, how he loved me!

LUKA.   Yes, yes, it's all right. I believe you! Patent leathers, you said?
Well, well, well—and you loved him, did you? [*Disappears with her
around the corner*]

THE BARON.   God—isn't she a fool, though? She's good-hearted—
but such a fool—it's past belief!

BUBNOFF.   And why are people so fond of lying—just as if they were
up before the judge—really!

NATASHA.   I guess lying is more fun than speaking the truth—I,
too . . .

THE BARON.   What—you, too? Go on!

NATASHA.   Oh—I imagine things—invent them—and I wait—

THE BARON.   For what?

NATASHA [*smiling confusedly*].   Oh—I think that perhaps—well—
to-morrow somebody will really appear—some one—oh—out of the
ordinary—or something'll happen—also out of the ordinary. . . . I've
been waiting for it—oh—always. . . . But, really, what is there to wait
for? [*Pause*]

THE BARON [*with a slight smile*].   Nothing—I expect nothing!
What is past, is past! Through! Over with! And then what?

NATASHA.   And then—well—to-morrow I imagine suddenly that I'll
die—and I get frightened . . . in summer it's all right to dream of
death—then there are thunder storms—one might get struck by light-
ning . . .

THE BARON.   You've a hard life . . . your sister's a wicked-tempered
devil!

NATASHA.   Tell me—does anybody live happily? It's hard for all of
us—I can see that . . .

KLESHTCH [*who until this moment has sat motionless and indifferent,
jumps up suddenly*].   For all? You lie! Not for all! If it were so—all
right! Then it wouldn't hurt—yes!

BUBNOFF.   What in hell's bit you? Just listen to him yelping!

[KLESHTCH *lies down again and grunts.*]

THE BARON.   Well—I'd better go and make my peace with
Nastinka—if I don't, she won't treat me to vodka . . .

BUBNOFF.   Hm—people love to lie . . . with Nastka—I can see the
reason why. She's used to painting that mutt of hers—and now she
wants to paint her soul as well . . . put rouge on her soul, eh? But the
others—why do they? Take Luka for instance—he lies a lot . . . and
what does he get out of it? He's an old fellow, too—why does he do it?

THE BARON [*smiling and walking away*].   All people have drab-
colored souls—and they like to brighten them up a bit . . .

LUKA [*appearing from round the corner*].   You, sir, why do you tease
the girl? Leave her alone—let her cry if it amuses her . . . she weeps for
her own pleasure—what harm is it to you?

THE BARON.   Nonsense, old man! She's a nuisance. Raoul to-day,
Gaston to-morrow—always the same old yarn, though! Still—I'll go
and make up with her. [*Leaves*]

LUKA.   That's right—go—and be nice to her. Being nice to people
never does them any harm . . .

NATASHA.   You're so good, little father—why are you so good?

LUKA.   Good, did you say? Well—call it that! [*Behind the brick wall
is heard soft singing and the sounds of a concertina*] Some one has to be
kind, girl—some one must pity people! Christ pitied everybody—and
he said to us: "Go and do likewise!" I tell you—if you pity a man when
he most needs it, good comes of it. Why—I used to be a watchman on
the estate of an engineer near Tomsk—all right—the house was right
in the middle of a forest—lovely place—winter came—and I remained
all by myself. Well—one night I heard a nosie—

NATASHA.   Thieves?

LUKA.   Exactly! Thieves creeping in! I took my gun—I went out. I
looked and saw two of them opening a window—and so busy that they
didn't even see me. I yell: "Hey there—get out of here!" And they turn
on me with their axes—I warn them to stand back, or I'd shoot—and
as I speak, I keep on covering them with my gun, first the one, then the
other—they go down on their knees, as if to implore me for mercy. And
by that time I was furious—because of those axes, you see—and so I say
to them: "I was chasing you, you scoundrels—and you didn't go. Now
you go and break off some stout branches!"—and they did so—and I
say: "Now—one of you lie down and let the other one flog him!" So
they obey me and flog each other—and then they begin to implore me
again. "Grandfather," they say, "for God's sake give us some bread!
We're hungry!" There's thieves for you, my dear! [*Laughs*] And with an

ax, too! Yes—honest peasants, both of them! And I say to them, "You should have asked for bread straight away!" And they say: "We got tired of asking—you beg and beg—and nobody gives you a crumb—it hurts!" So they stayed with me all that winter—one of them, Stepan, would take my gun and go shooting in the forest—and the other, Yakoff, was ill most of the time—he coughed a lot . . . and so the three of us together looked after the house . . . then spring came . . . "Goodbye, grandfather," they said—and they went away—back home to Russia . . .

NATASHA.   Were they escaped convicts?

LUKA.   That's just what they were—escaped convicts—from a Siberian prison camp . . . honest peasants! If I hadn't felt sorry for them—they might have killed me—or maybe worse—and then there would have been trial and prison and afterwards Siberia—what's the sense of it? Prison teaches no good—and Siberia doesn't either—but another human being can . . . yes, a human being can teach another one kindness—very simply! [*Pause*]

BUBNOFF.   Hm—yes—I, for instance, don't know how to lie . . . why—as far as I'm concerned, I believe in coming out with the whole truth and putting it on thick . . . why fuss about it?

KLESHTCH [*again jumps up as if his clothes were on fire, and screams*].   What truth? Where is there truth? [*Tearing at his ragged clothes*] Here's truth for you! No work! No strength! That's the only truth! Shelter—there's no shelter! You die—that's the truth! Hell! What do I want with the truth? Let me breathe! Why should I be blamed? What do I want with truth? To live—Christ Almighty!—they won't let you live—and that's another truth!

BUBNOFF.   He's mad!

LUKA.   Dear Lord . . . listen to me, brother—

KLESHTCH [*trembling with excitement*].   They say: there's truth! You, old man, try to console every one . . . I tell you—I hate every one! And there's your truth—God curse it—understand? I tell you—God curse it!

[*Rushes away round the corner, turning as he goes.*]

LUKA.   Ah—how excited he got! Where did he run off to?

NATASHA.   He's off his head . . .

BUBNOFF.   God—don't he say a whole lot, though? As if he was playing drama—he gets those fits often . . . he isn't used to life yet . . .

PEPEL [*comes slowly round the corner*].   Peace on all this honest gathering! Well, Luka, you wily old fellow—still telling them stories?

LUKA.   You should have heard how that fellow carried on!

PEPEL.   Kleshtch—wasn't it? What's wrong with him? He was running like one possessed!

LUKA.   You'd do the same if your own heart were breaking!

PEPEL [*sitting down*].   I don't like him . . . he's got such a nasty, bad temper—and so proud! [*Imitating* KLESHTCH] "I'm a workman!" And he thinks everyone's beneath him. Go on working if you feel like it—nothing to be so damned haughty about! If work is the standard—a horse can give us points—pulls like hell and says nothing! Natasha—are your folks at home?

NATASHA.   They went to the cemetery—then to night service . . .

PEPEL.   So that's why you're free for once—quite a novelty!

LUKA [*to* BUBNOFF, *thoughtfully*].   There—you say—truth! Truth doesn't always heal a wounded soul. For instance, I knew of a man who believed in a land of righteousness . . .

BUBNOFF.   In what?

LUKA.   In a land of righteousness. He said: "Somewhere on this earth there must be a righteous land—and wonderful people live there—good people! They respect each other, help each other, and everything is peaceful and good!" And so that man—who was always searching for this land of righteousness—he was poor and lived miserably—and when things got to be so bad with him that it seemed there was nothing else for him to do except lie down and die—even then he never lost heart—but he'd just smile and say: "Never mind! I can stand it! A little while longer—and I'll have done with this life—and I'll go in search of the righteous land!"—it was his one happiness—the thought of that land . . .

PEPEL.   Well? Did he go there?

BUBNOFF.   Where? Ho-ho!

LUKA.   And then to this place—in Siberia, by the way—there came a convict—a learned man with books and maps—yes, a learned man who knew all sorts of things—and the other man said to him: "Do me a favor—show me where is the land of righteousness and how I can get there." At once the learned man opened his books, spread out his maps, and looked and looked and he said—no—he couldn't find this land anywhere . . . everything was correct—all the lands on earth were marked—but not this land of righteousness . . .

PEPEL [*in a low voice*].   Well? Wasn't there a trace of it?

[BUBNOFF *roars with laughter.*]

NATASHA.   Wait . . . well, little father?

LUKA.   The man wouldn't believe it. . . . "It must exist," he said, "look carefully. Otherwise," he says, "your books and maps are of no use if there's no land of righteousness." The learned man was offended.

"My plans," he said, "are correct. But there exists no land of righteousness anywhere." Well, then the other man got angry. He'd lived and lived and suffered and suffered, and had believed all the time in the existence of this land—and now, according to the plans, it didn't exist at all. He felt robbed! And he said to the learned man: "Ah—you scum of the earth! You're not a learned man at all—but just a damned cheat!"—and he gave him a good wallop in the eye—then another one . . . [*After a moment's silence*] And then he went home and hanged himself!

[*All are silent.* LUKA, *smiling, looks at* PEPEL *and* NATASHA.]

PEPEL [*low-voiced*].   To hell with this story—it isn't very cheerful . . .

NATASHA.   He couldn't stand the disappointment . . .

BUBNOFF [*sullen*].   Ah—it's nothing but a fairytale . . .

PEPEL.   Well—there is the righteous land for you—doesn't exist, it seems . . .

NATASHA.   I'm sorry for that man . . .

BUBNOFF.   All a story—ho-ho!—land of righteousness—what an idea! [*Exits through window*]

LUKA [*pointing to window*].   He's laughing! [*Pause*] Well, children, God be with you! I'll leave you soon . . .

PEPEL.   Where are you going to?

LUKA.   To the Ukraine—I heard they discovered a new religion there—I want to see—yes! People are always seeking—they always want something better—God grant them patience!

PEPEL.   You think they'll find it?

LUKA.   The people? They will find it! He who seeks, will find! He who desires strongly, will find!

NATASHA.   If only they could find something better—invent something better . . .

LUKA.   They're trying to! But we must help them girl—we must respect them . . .

NATASHA.   How can I help them? I am helpless myself!

PEPEL [*determined*].   Again—listen—I'll speak to you again, Natasha—here—before him—he knows everything . . . run away with me?

NATASHA.   Where? From one prison to another?

PEPEL.   I told you—I'm through with being a thief, so help me God! I'll quit! If I say so, I'll do it! I can read and write—I'll work—He's been telling me to go to Siberia on my own hook—let's go there together, what do you say? Do you think I'm not disgusted with my life? Oh—Natasha—I know . . . I see . . . I console myself with the thought that there are lots of people who are honored and respected—and who are bigger thieves than I! But what good is that to me? It isn't that I repent . . . I've no conscience . . . but I do feel one thing: One must live differently. One must live a better life . . . one must be able to respect one's own self . . .

LUKA. That's right, friend! May God help you! It's true! A man must respect himself!

PEPEL. I've been a thief from childhood on. Everybody always called me "Vaska—the thief—the son of a thief!" Oh—very well then—I am a thief . . . just imagine—now, perhaps, I'm a thief out of spite—perhaps I'm a thief because no one ever called me anything different. . . . Well, Natasha—?

NATASHA [*sadly*]. Somehow I don't believe in words—and I'm restless to-day—my heart is heavy . . . as if I were expecting something . . . it's a pity, Vassily, that you talked to me to-day . . .

PEPEL. When should I? It isn't the first time I speak to you . . .

NATASHA. And why should I go with you? I don't love you so very much—sometimes I like you—and other times the mere sight of you makes me sick . . . it seems—no—I don't really love you . . . when one really loves, one sees no fault. . . . But I do see . . .

PEPEL. Never mind—you'll love me after a while! I'll make you care for me . . . if you'll just say yes! For over a year I've watched you . . . you're a decent girl . . . you're kind—you're reliable—I'm very much in love with you . . .

[VASSILISA, *in her best dress, appears at window and listens.*]

NATASHA. Yes—you love me—but how about my sister . . . ?

PEPEL [*confused*]. Well, what of her? There are plenty like her . . .

LUKA. You'll be all right, girl! If there's no bread, you have to eat weeds . . .

PEPEL [*gloomily*]. Please—feel a little sorry for me! My life isn't all roses—it's a hell of a life . . . little happiness in it . . . I feel as if a swamp were sucking me under . . . and whatever I try to catch and hold on to, is rotten . . . it breaks . . . Your sister—oh—I thought she was different . . . if she weren't so greedy after money . . . I'd have done anything for her sake, if she were only all mine . . . but she must have someone else . . . and she has to have money—and freedom . . . because she doesn't like the straight and narrow . . . she can't help me. But you're like a young fir-tree . . . you bend, but you don't break . . .

LUKA. Yes—go with him, girl, go! He's a good lad—he's all right! Only tell him every now and then that he's a good lad so that he won't forget it—and he'll believe you. Just you keep on telling him "Vasya, you're a good man—don't you forget it!" Just think, dear, where else could you go except with him? Your sister is a savage beast . . . and as

for her husband, there's little to say of him. He's rotten beyond words
. . . and all this life here, where will it get you? But this lad is strong . . .

NATASHA.   Nowhere to go—I know—I thought of it. The only thing
is—I've no faith in anybody—and there's no place for me to turn to . . .

PEPEL.   Yes, there is! But I won't let you go that way—I'd rather cut
your throat!

NATASHA [*smiling*].   There—I'm not his wife yet—and he talks already of killing me!

PEPEL [*puts his arms around her*].   Come, Natasha! Say yes!

NATASHA [*holding him close*].   But I'll tell you one thing, Vassily—
I swear it before God . . . the first time you strike me or hurt me any
other way, I'll have no pity on myself . . . I'll either hang myself . . .
or . . .

PEPEL.   May my hand wither if ever I touch you!

LUKA.   Don't doubt him, dear! He needs you more than you need
him!

VASSILISA [*from the window*].   So now they're engaged! Love and advice!

NATASHA.   They've come back—oh, God—they saw—oh,
Vassily . . .

PEPEL.   Why are you frightened? Nobody'll dare touch you now!

VASSILISA.   Don't be afraid, Natalia! He won't beat you . . . he don't
know how to love or how to beat . . . I know!

LUKA [*in a low voice*].   Rotten old hag—like a snake in the grass . . .

VASSILISA.   He dares only with the word!

KOSTILYOFF [*enters*].   Natashka! What are you doing here, you parasite? Gossiping? Kicking about your family? And the samovar not
ready? And the table not cleared?

NATASHA [*going out*].   I thought you were going to church . . . ?

KOSTILYOFF.   None of your business what we intended doing! Mind
your own affairs—and do what you're told!

PEPEL.   Shut up, you! She's no longer your servant! Don't go,
Natalia—don't do a thing!

NATASHA.   Stop ordering me about—you're commencing too soon!
[*Leaves*]

PEPEL [*to* KOSTILYOFF].   That's enough. You've used her long
enough—now she's mine!

KOSTILYOFF.   Yours? When did you buy her—and for how much?

[VASSILISA *roars with laughter.*]

LUKA.   Go away, Vasya!

PEPEL.   Don't laugh, you fools—or first thing you know I'll make
you cry!

VASSILISA.   Oh, how terrible! Oh—how you frighten me!

LUKA.   Vassily—go away! Don't you see—she's goading you on . . . ridiculing you, don't you understand . . . ?

PEPEL.   Yes . . . You lie, lie! You won't get what you want!

VASSILISA.   Nor will I get what I don't want, Vasya!

PEPEL [*shaking his fist at her*].   We'll see . . . [*Exits*]

VASSILISA [*disappearing through window*].   I'll arrange some wedding for you . . .

KOSTILYOFF [*crossing to* LUKA].   Well, old man, how's everything?

LUKA.   All right!

KOSTILYOFF.   You're going away, they say—?

LUKA.   Soon.

KOSTILYOFF.   Where to?

LUKA.   I'll follow my nose . . .

KOSTILYOFF.   Tramping, eh? Don't like stopping in one place all the time, do you?

LUKA.   Even water won't pass beneath a stone that's sunk too firmly in the ground, they say . . .

KOSTILYOFF.   That's true for a stone. But man must settle in one place. Men can't live like cockroaches, crawling about wherever they want. . . . A man must stick to one place—and not wander about aimlessly . . .

LUKA.   But suppose his home is wherever he hangs his hat?

KOSTILYOFF.   Why, then—he's a vagabond—useless . . . a human being must be of some sort of use—he must work . . .

LUKA.   That's what you think, eh?

KOSTILYOFF.   Yes—sure . . . just look! What's a vagabond? A strange fellow . . . unlike all others. If he's a real pilgrim then he's some good in the world . . . perhaps he discovered a new truth. Well—but not every truth is worth while. Let him keep it to himself and shut up about it! Or else—let him speak in a way which no one can understand . . . don't let him interfere . . . don't let him stir up people without cause! It's none of his business how other people live! Let him follow his own righteous path . . . in the woods—or in a monastery—away from everybody! He mustn't interfere—nor condemn other people—but pray— pray for all of us—for all the world's sins—for mine—for yours— for everybody's. To pray—that's why he forsakes the world's turmoil! That's so! [*Pause*] But you—what sort of a pilgrim are you—? An honest person must have a passport . . . all honest people have passports . . . yes . . . !

LUKA.   In this world there are people—and also just plain men . . .

KOSTILYOFF.   Don't coin wise sayings! Don't give me riddles! I'm as clever as you . . . what's the difference—people and men?

LUKA. What riddle is there? I say—there's sterile and there's fertile ground . . . whatever you sow in it, grows . . . that's all . . .

KOSTILYOFF. What do you mean?

LUKA. Take yourself for instance . . . if the Lord God himself said to you: "Mikhailo, be a man!"—it would be useless—nothing would come of it—you're doomed to remain just as you are . . .

KOSTILYOFF. Oh—but do you realize that my wife's uncle is a policeman, and that if I . . .

VASSILISA [coming in]. Mikhail Ivanitch—come and have your tea . . .

KOSTILYOFF [to LUKA]. You listen! Get out! You leave this place—hear?

VASSILISA. Yes—get out, old man! Your tongue's too long! And—who knows—you may be an escaped convict . . .

KOSTILYOFF. If I ever see sign of you again after to-day—well—I've warned you!

LUKA. You'll call your uncle, eh? Go on—call him! Tell him you've caught an escaped convict—and maybe uncle'll get a reward—perhaps all of three kopecks . . .

BUBNOFF [in the window]. What are you bargaining about? Three kopecks—for what?

LUKA. They're threatening to sell me . . .

VASSILISA [to her husband]. Come . . .

BUBNOFF. For three kopecks? Well—look out, old man—they may even do it for one!

KOSTILYOFF [to BUBNOFF]. You have a habit of jumping up like a jack-in-the-box!

VASSILISA. The world is full of shady people and crooks—

LUKA. Hope you'll enjoy your tea!

VASSILISA [turning]. Shut up! You rotten toadstool!

[Leaves with her husband.]

LUKA. I'm off to-night.

BUBNOFF. That's right. Don't outstay your welcome!

LUKA. True enough.

BUBNOFF. I know. Perhaps I've escaped the gallows by getting away in time . . .

LUKA. Well?

BUBNOFF. That's true. It was this way. My wife took up with my boss. He was great at his trade—could dye a dog's skin so that it looked like a raccoon's—could change cat's skin into kangaroo—muskrats, all sorts of things. Well—my wife took up with him—and they were so mad about each other that I got afraid they might poison me or some-

thing like that—so I commenced beating up my wife—and the boss
beat me . . . we fought savagely! Once he tore off half my whiskers—
and broke one of my ribs . . . well, then I, too, got enraged. . . . I cracked
my wife over the head with an iron yard-measure—well—and alto-
gether it was like an honest-to-God war! And then I saw that nothing really could come of it . . . they were planning to get the best of me! So
I started planning—how to kill my wife—I thought of it a whole lot . . .
but I thought better of it just in time . . . and got away . . .

LUKA.   That was best! Let them go on changing dogs into raccoons!

BUBNOFF.   Only—the shop was in my wife's name . . . and so I did
myself out of it, you see? Although, to tell the truth, I would have drunk
it away . . . I'm a hard drinker, you know . . .

LUKA.   A hard drinker—oh . . .

BUBNOFF.   The worst you ever met! Once I start drinking, I drink
everything in sight, I'll spend every bit of money I have—everything except my bones and my skin . . . what's more, I'm lazy . . . it's terrible
how I hate work!

[*Enter* SATINE *and* THE ACTOR, *quarreling.*]

SATINE.   Nonsense! You'll go nowhere—it's all a damned lie! Old
man, what did you stuff him with all those fairytales for?

THE ACTOR.   You lie! Grandfather! Tell him that he lies!—I am
going away. I worked to-day—I swept the streets . . . and I didn't have a
drop of vodka. What do you think of that? Here they are—two fifteen
kopeck pieces—and I'm sober!

SATINE.   Why—that's absurd! Give it to me—I'll either drink it
up—or lose it at cards . . .

THE ACTOR.   Get out—this is for my journey . . .

LUKA [*to* SATINE].   And you—why are you trying to lead him astray?

SATINE.   Tell me, soothsayer, beloved by the Gods, what's my future
going to be? I've gone to pieces, brother—but everything isn't lost
yet, grandfather . . . there are sharks in this world who got more brains
than I!

LUKA.   You're cheerful, Constantine—and very agreeable!

BUBNOFF.   Actor, come over here! [THE ACTOR *crosses to window,
sits down on the sill before* BUBNOFF, *and speaks in a low voice with him*]

SATINE.   You know, brother, I used to be a clever youngster. It's nice
to think of it. I was a devil of a fellow . . . danced splendidly, played on
the stage, loved to amuse people . . . it was awfully gay . . .

LUKA.   How did you get to be what you are?

SATINE.   You're inquisitive, old man! You want to know everything?
What for?

LUKA.   I want to understand the ways of men—I look at you, and I

don't understand. You're a bold lad, Constantine, and you're no fool
. . . yet, all of a sudden . . .

SATINE.   It's prison, grandfather—I spent four years and seven
months in prison—afterwards—where could I go?

LUKA.   Aha! What were you there for?

SATINE.   On account of a scoundrel—whom I killed in a fit of rage
. . . and despair . . . and in prison I learned to play cards . . .

LUKA.   You killed—because of a woman?

SATINE.   Because of my own sister. . . . But look here—leave me
alone! I don't care for these cross-examinations—and all this happened
a long time ago. It's already nine years since my sister's death. . . .
Brother, she was a wonderful girl . . .

LUKA.   You take life easily! And only a while ago that locksmith was
here—and how he did yell!

SATINE.   Kleshtch?

LUKA.   Yes—"There's no work," he shouted; "there isn't anything . . ."

SATINE.   He'll get used to it. What could I do?

LUKA [softly].   Look—here he comes!

[KLESHTCH walks in slowly, his head bowed low.]

SATINE.   Hey, widower! Why are you so down in the mouth? What
are you thinking?

KLESHTCH.   I'm thinking—what'll I do? I've no food—nothing—
the funeral ate up all . . .

SATINE.   I'll give you a bit of advice . . . do nothing! Just be a burden to the world at large!

KLESHTCH.   Go on—talk—I'd be ashamed of myself . . .

SATINE.   Why—people aren't ashamed to let you live worse than a
dog. Just think . . . you stop work—so do I—so do hundreds, thousands
of others—everybody—understand?—Everybody'll quit working . . .
nobody'll do a damned thing—and then what'll happen?

KLESHTCH.   They'll all starve to death . . .

LUKA [to SATINE].   If those are your notions, you ought to join the
order of Begunes—you know—there's some such organization . . .

SATINE.   I know—grandfather—and they're no fools . . .

[NATASHA is heard screaming behind KOSTILYOFF's window: "What
for? Stop! What have I done?"]

LUKA [worried].   Natasha! That was she crying—oh, God . . .

[From KOSTILYOFF's room is heard noise, shuffling, breaking of
crockery, and KOSTILYOFF's shrill cry: "Ah! Heretic! Bitch!"]

VASSILISA.   Wait, wait—I'll teach her—there, there!

NATASHA.   They're beating me—killing me . . .

SATINE [*shouts through the window*].   Hey—you there . . .

LUKA [*trembling*].   Where's Vassily—? Call Vaska—oh, God—listen, brothers . . .

THE ACTOR [*running out*].   I'll find him at once!

BUBNOFF.   They beat her a lot these days . . .

SATINE.   Come on, old man—we'll be witnesses . . .

LUKA [*following* SATINE].   Oh—witnesses—what for? Vassily—he should be called at once!

NATASHA.   Sister—sister dear! Va-a-a . . .

BUBNOFF.   They've gagged her—I'll go and see . . .

> [*The noise in* KOSTILYOFF's *room dies down gradually as if they had gone into the hallway. The old man's cry: "Stop!" is heard. A door is slammed noisily, and the latter sound cuts off all the other noises sharply. Quiet on the stage. Twilight.*]

KLESHTCH [*seated on the sledge, indifferently, rubbing his hands; mutters at first indistinguishably, then:*] What then? One must live. [*Louder*] Must have shelter—well? There's no shelter, no roof—nothing . . . there's only man—man alone—no hope . . . no help . . .

> [*Exit slowly, his head bent. A few moments of ominous silence, then somewhere in the hallway a mass of sounds, which grows in volume and comes nearer. Individual voices are heard.*]

VASSILISA.   I'm her sister—let go . . .

KOSTILYOFF.   What right have you . . . ?

VASSILISA.   Jail-bird!

SATINE.   Call Vaska—quickly! Zob—hit him!

> [*A police whistle.* THE TARTAR *runs in, his right hand in a sling.*]

THE TARTAR.   There's a new law for you—kill only in daytime!

> [*Enter* ZOB, *followed by* MIEDVIEDIEFF.]

ZOB.   I handed him a good one!

MIEDVIEDIEFF.   You—how dare you fight?

THE TARTAR.   What about yourself? What's your duty?

MIEDVIEDIEFF [*running after*].   Stop—give back my whistle!

KOSTILYOFF [*runs in*].   Abram! Stop him! Hold him! He's a murderer—he . . .

> [*Enter* KVASHNYA *and* NASTYA *supporting* NATASHA *who is disheveled.* SATINE *backs away, pushing away* VASSILISA *who is try-*

ing to attack her sister, while, near her, ALYOSHKA *jumps up and down like a madman, whistles into her ear, shrieking, roaring. Also other ragged men and women.*]

SATINE [*to* VASSILISA].   Well—you damned bitch!

VASSILISA.   Let go, you jail-bird! I'll tear you to pieces—if I have to pay for it with my own life!

KVASHNYA [*leading* NATASHA *aside*].   You—Karpovna—that's enough—stand back—aren't you ashamed? Or are you crazy?

MIEDVIEDIEFF [*seizes* SATINE].   Aha—caught at last!

SATINE.   Zob—beat them up! Vaska—Vaska . . .

[*They all, in a chaotic mass, struggle near the brick wall. They lead* NATASHA *to the right, and set her on a pile of wood.* PEPEL *rushes in from the hallway and, silently, with powerful movements, pushes the crowd aside.*]

PEPEL.   Natalia, where are you . . . you . . .

KOSTILYOFF [*disappearing behind a corner*].   Abram! Seize Vaska! Comrades—help us get him! The thief! The robber!

PEPEL.   You—you old bastard! [*Aiming a terrific blow at* KOSTILYOFF. KOSTILYOFF *falls so that only the upper part of his body is seen.* PEPEL *rushes to* NATASHA]

VASSILISA.   Beat Vaska! Brothers! Beat the thief!

MIEDVIEDIEFF [*yells to* SATINE].   Keep out of this—it's a family affair . . . they're relatives . . . and who are you . . .

PEPEL [*to* NATASHA].   What did she do to you? She used a knife?

KVASHNYA.   God—what beasts! They've scalded the child's feet with boiling water!

NASTYA.   They overturned the samovar . . .

THE TARTAR.   Maybe an accident—you must make sure—you can't exactly tell . . .

NATASHA [*half fainting*].   Vassily—take me away—

VASSILISA.   Good people! Come! Look! He's dead! Murdered!

[*All crowd into the hallway near* KOSTILYOFF. BUBNOFF *leaves the crowd and crosses to* PEPEL.]

BUBNOFF [*in a low voice, to* PEPEL].   Vaska—the old man is done for!

PEPEL [*looks at him, as though he does not understand*].   Go—for help—she must be taken to the hospital . . . I'll settle with them . . .

BUBNOFF.   I say—the old man—somebody's killed him . . .

[*The noise on the stage dies out like a fire under water. Distinct, whispered exclamations:* "Not really?" "Well—let's go away,

brothers!" "The devil!" "Hold on now!" "Let's get away before the
police comes!" The crowd disappears. BUBNOFF, THE TARTAR,
NASTYA, and KVASHNYA, rush up to KOSTILYOFF's body.]

VASSILISA [rises and cries out triumphantly].   Killed—my husband's
killed! Vaska killed him! I saw him! Brothers, I saw him! Well—
Vasya—the police!

PEPEL [moves away from NATASHA].   Let me alone. [Looks at
KOSTILYOFF; to VASSILISA] Well—are you glad? [Touches the corpse with
his foot] The old bastard is dead! Your wish has been granted! Why not
do the same to you? [Throws himself at her]

[SATINE and ZOB quickly overpower him, and VASSILISA disappears
in the passage.]

SATINE.   Come to your senses!

ZOB.   Hold on! Not so fast!

VASSILISA [appearing].   Well, Vaska, dear friend? You can't escape
your fate. . . . police—Abram—whistle!

MIEDVIEDIEFF.   Those devils tore my whistle off!

ALYOSHKA.   Here it is! [Whistles, MIEDVIEDIEFF runs after him]

SATINE [leading PEPEL to NATASHA].   Don't be afraid, Vaska! Killed
in a row! That's nonsense—only manslaughter—you won't have to
serve a long term . . .

VASSILISA.   Hold Vaska—he killed him—I saw it!

SATINE.   I, too, gave the old man a couple of blows—he was easily
fixed . . . you call me as witness, Vaska!

PEPEL.   I don't need to defend myself . . . I want to drag Vassilisa
into this mess—and I'll do it—she was the one who wanted it . . . she
was the one who urged me to kill him—she goaded me on . . .

NATASHA [sudden and loud].   Oh—I understand—so that's it,
Vassily? Good people! They're both guilty—my sister and he—they're
both guilty! They had it all planned! So, Vassily, that's why you spoke
to me a while ago—so that she should overhear everything—? Good
people! She's his mistress—you know it—everybody knows it—they're
both guilty! She—she urged him to kill her husband—he was in their
way—and so was I! And now they've maimed me . . .

PEPEL.   Natalia! What's the matter with you? What are you saying?

SATINE.   Oh—hell!

VASSILISA.   You lie. She lies. He—Vaska killed him . . .

NATASHA.   They're both guilty! God damn you both!

SATINE.   What a mix-up! Hold on, Vassily—or they'll ruin you between them!

ZOB.   I can't understand it—oh—what a mess!

PEPEL.   Natalia! It can't be true! Surely you don't believe that I—with her—

SATINE.   So help me God, Natasha! Just think . . .

VASSILISA [*in the passage*].   They've killed my husband—Your Excellency! Vaska Pepel, the thief, killed him, Captain! I saw it—everybody saw it . . .

NATASHA [*tossing about in agony; her mind wandering*].   Good people—my sister and Vaska killed him! The police—listen—this sister of mine—here—she urged, coaxed her lover—there he stands—the scoundrel! They both killed him! Put them in jail! Bring them before the judge! Take me along, too! To prison! Christ Almighty—take me to prison, too!

CURTAIN

Act IV

Same as Act I. But PEPEL's *room is no longer there, and the partition has been removed. Furthermore, there is no anvil at the place where* KLESHTCH *used to sit and work. In the corner, where* PEPEL's *room used to be,* THE TARTAR *lies stretched out, rather restless, and groaning from time to time.* KLESHTCH *sits at one end of the table, repairing a concertina and now and then testing the stops. At the other end of the table sits* SATINE, THE BARON, *and* NASTYA. *In front of them stand a bottle of vodka, three bottles of beer, and a large loaf of black bread.* THE ACTOR *lies on top of the stove, shifting about and coughing. It is night. The stage is lit by a lamp in the middle of the table. Outside the wind howls.*

KLESHTCH. Yes . . . he disappeared during the confusion and noise . . .

THE BARON. He vanished under the very eyes of the police—just like a puff of smoke . . .

SATINE. That's how sinners flee from the company of the righteous!

NASTYA. He was a dear old soul! But you—you aren't men—you're just—oh—like rust on iron!

THE BARON [*drinks*]. Here's to you, my lady!

SATINE. He was an inquisitive old fellow—yes! Nastenka here fell in love with him . . .

NASTYA. Yes! I did! Madly! It's true! He saw everything—understood everything . . .

SATINE [*laughing*]. Yes, generally speaking, I would say that he was—oh—like mush to those who can't chew . . .

THE BARON [*laughing*]. Right! Like plaster on a boil!

55

KLESHTCH.   He was merciful—you people don't know what pity means . . .

SATINE.   What good can I do you by pitying you?

KLESHTCH.   You needn't have pity—but you needn't harm or offend your fellow-beings, either!

THE TARTAR [*sits up on his bunk, nursing his wounded hand carefully*].   He was a fine old man. The law of life was the law of his heart. . . . And he who obeys this law, is good, while he who disregards it, perishes . . .

THE BARON.   What law, Prince?

THE TARTAR.   There are a number—different ones—you know . . .

THE BARON.   Proceed!

THE TARTAR.   Do not do harm unto others—such is the law!

SATINE.   Oh—you mean the Penal Code, criminal and correctional, eh?

THE BARON.   And also the Code of Penalties inflicted by Justices of the Peace!

THE TARTAR.   No. I mean the Koran. It is the supreme law—and your own soul ought to be the Koran—yes!

KLESHTCH [*testing his concertina*].   It wheezes like all hell! But the Prince speaks the truth—one must live abiding by the law—by the teachings of the Gospels . . .

SATINE.   Well—go ahead and do it!

THE BARON.   Just try it!

THE TARTAR.   The Prophet Mohammed gave to us the law. He said: "Here is the law! Do as it is written therein!" Later on a time will arrive when the Koran will have outlived its purpose—and time will bring forth its own laws—every generation will create its own . . .

SATINE.   To be sure! Time passed on—and gave us—the Criminal Code . . . It's a strong law, brother—it won't wear off so very soon!

NASTYA [*banging her glass on the table*].   Why—why do I stay here—with you? I'll go away somewhere—to the ends of the world!

THE BARON.   Without any shoes, my lady?

NASTYA.   I'll go—naked, if must be—creeping on all fours!

THE BARON.   That'll be rather picturesque, my lady—on all fours!

NASTYA.   Yes—and I'll crawl if I have to—anything at all—as long as I don't have to see your faces any longer—oh, I'm so sick of it all—the life—the people—everything!

SATINE.   When you go, please take the actor along—he's preparing to go to the very same place—he has learned that within a half mile's distance of the end of the world there's a hospital for diseased organons . . .

THE ACTOR [*raising his head over the top of the stove*].   A hospital for organisms—you fool!

SATINE.   For organons—poisoned with vodka!

THE ACTOR.   Yes! He will go! He will indeed! You'll see!

THE BARON.   Who is he, sir?

THE ACTOR.   I!

THE BARON.   Thanks, servant of the goddess—what's her name—? The goddess of drama—tragedy—whatever is her name—?

THE ACTOR.   The muse, idiot! Not the goddess—the muse!

SATINE.   Lachesis—Hera—Aphrodite—Atropos—oh! To hell with them all! You see—Baron—it was the old man who stuffed the actor's head full with this rot . . .

THE BARON.   That old man's a fool . . .

THE ACTOR.   Ignoramuses! Beasts! Melpomene—that's her name! Heartless brutes! Bastards! You'll see! He'll go! "On with the orgy, dismal spirits!"—poem—ah—by Béranger! Yes—he'll find some spot where there's no—no . . .

THE BARON.   Where there's nothing, sir?

THE ACTOR.   Right! Nothing! "This hole shall be my grave—I am dying—ill and exhausted . . ." Why do you exist? Why?

THE BARON.   You! God or genius or orgy—or whatever you are—don't roar so loud!

THE ACTOR.   You lie! I'll roar all I want to!

NASTYA [*lifting her head from the table and throwing up her hands*]. Go on! Yell! Let them listen to you!

THE BARON.   Where is the sense, my lady?

SATINE.   Leave them alone, Baron! To hell with the lot! Let them yell—let them knock their damned heads off if they feel like it! There's a method in their madness! Don't you go and interfere with people as that old fellow did! Yes—it's he—the damned old fool—he bewitched the whole gang of us!

KLESHTCH.   He persuaded them to go away—but failed to show them the road . . .

THE BARON.   That old man was a humbug!

NASTYA.   Liar! You're a humbug yourself!

THE BARON.   Shut up, my lady!

KLESHTCH.   The old man didn't like truth very much—as a matter of fact, he strongly resented it—and wasn't he right, though? Just look—where is there any truth? And yet, without it, you can't breathe! For instance, our Tartar Prince over there, crushed his hand at his work—and now he'll have to have his arm amputated—and there's the truth for you!

SATINE [*striking the table with his clenched fist*].   Shut up! You sons

of bitches! Fools! Not another word about that old fellow! [*To* THE
BARON] You, Baron, are the worst of the lot! You don't understand a
thing, and you lie like the devil! The old man's no humbug! What's the
truth? Man! Man—that's the truth! He understood man—you don't!
You're all as dumb as stones! I understand the old man—yes! He lied—
but lied out of sheer pity for you . . . God damn you! Lots of people lie
out of pity for their fellow-beings! I know! I've read about it! They lie—
oh—beautifully, inspiringly, stirringly! Some lies bring comfort, and
others bring peace—a lie alone can justify the burden which crushed
a workman's hand and condemns those who are starving! I know what
lying means! The weakling and the one who is a parasite through his
very weakness—they both need lies—lies are their support, their shield,
their armor! But the man who is strong, who is his own master, who is
free and does not have to suck his neighbors' blood—he needs no lies!
To lie—it's the creed of slaves and masters of slaves! Truth is the religion of the free man!

THE BARON.   Bravo! Well spoken! Hear, hear! I agree! You speak
like an honest man!

SATINE.   And why can't a crook at times speak the truth—since
honest people at times speak like crooks? Yes—I've forgotten a lot—but
I still know a thing or two! The old man? Oh—he's wise! He affected
me as acid affects a dirty old silver coin! Let's drink to his health! Fill
the glasses . . . [NASTYA *fills a glass with beer and hands it to* SATINE,
who laughs] The old man lives within himself . . . he looks upon all the
world from his own angle. Once I asked him: "Grand-dad, why do people live?" [*Tries to imitate* LUKA's *voice and gestures*] And he replied:
"Why, my dear fellow, people live in the hope of something better! For
example—let's say there are carpenters in this world, and all sorts of
trash . . . people . . . and they give birth to a carpenter the like of which
has never been seen upon the face of the earth . . . he's way above everybody else, and has no equal among carpenters! The brilliancy of his
personality was reflected on all his trade, on all the other carpenters, so
that they advanced twenty years in one day! This applies to all other
trades—blacksmiths and shoemakers and other workmen—and all the
peasants—and even the aristocrats live in the hopes of a higher life!
Each individual thinks that he's living for his own Self, but in reality he
lives in the hope of something better. A hundred years—sometimes
longer—do we expect, live for the finer, higher life . . ." [NASTYA *stares
intently into* SATINE's *face.* KLESHTCH *stops working and listens.* THE
BARON *bows his head very low, drumming softly on the table with his fin-
gers.* THE ACTOR, *peering down from the stove, tries to climb noiselessly
into the bunk*] "Every one, brothers, every one lives in the hope of
something better. That's why we must respect each and every human

being! How do we know who he is, why he was born, and what he is capable of accomplishing? Perhaps his coming into the world will prove to be our good fortune . . . Especially must we respect little children! Children—need freedom! Don't interfere with their lives! Respect children!" [*Pause*]

THE BARON [*thoughtfully*].   Hm—yes—something better?—That reminds me of my family . . . an old family dating back to the time of Catherine . . . all noblemen, soldiers, originally French . . . they served their country and gradually rose higher and higher. In the days of Nicholas the First my grandfather, Gustave DeBille, held a high post— riches—hundreds of serfs . . . horses—cooks—

NASTYA.   You liar! It isn't true!

THE BARON [*jumping up*].   What? Well—go on—

NASTYA.   It isn't true.

THE BARON [*screams*].   A house in Moscow! A house in Petersburg! Carriages! Carriages with coats of arms!

> [KLESHTCH *takes his concertina and goes to one side, watching the scene with interest.*]

NASTYA.   You lie!

THE BARON.   Shut up!—I say—dozens of footmen . . .

NASTYA [*delighted*].   You lie!

THE BARON.   I'll kill you!

NASTYA [*ready to run away*].   There were no carriages!

SATINE.   Stop, Nastenka! Don't infuriate him!

THE BARON.   Wait—you bitch! My grandfather . . .

NASTYA.   There was no grandfather! There was nothing!

> [SATINE *roars with laughter.*]

THE BARON [*worn out with rage, sits down on bench*].   Satine! Tell that slut—what—? You, too, are laughing? You—don't believe me either? [*Cries out in despair, pounding the table with his fists*] It's true— damn the whole lot of you!

NASTYA [*triumphantly*].   So—you're crying? Understand now what a human being feels like when nobody believes him?

KLESHTCH [*returning to the table*].   I thought there'd be a fight . . .

THE TARTAR.   Oh—people are fools! It's too bad . . .

THE BARON.   I shall not permit any one to ridicule me! I have proofs—documents—damn you!

SATINE.   Forget it! Forget about your grandfather's carriages! You can't drive anywhere in a carriage of the past!

THE BARON.   How dare she—just the same—?

NASTYA.   Just imagine! How dare I—?

SATINE. You see—she does dare! How is she any worse than you are? Although, surely, in her past there wasn't even a father and mother, let alone carriages and a grandfather . . .

THE BARON [*quieting down*].   Devil take you—you do know how to argue dispassionately—and I, it seems—I've no will-power . . .

SATINE. Acquire some—it's useful . . . [*Pause*] Nastya! Are you going to the hospital?

NASTYA. What for?

SATINE. To see Natashka.

NASTYA. Oh—just woke up, did you? She's been out of the hospital for some time—and they can't find a trace of her . . .

SATINE. Oh—that woman's a goner!

KLESHTCH.   It's interesting to see whether Vaska will get the best of Vassilisa, or the other way around—

NASTYA. Vassilisa will win out! She's shrewd! And Vaska will go to the gallows!

SATINE. For manslaughter? No—only to jail . . .

NASTYA. Too bad—the gallows would have been better . . . that's where all of you should be sent . . . swept off into a hole—like filth . . .

SATINE [*astonished*].   What's the matter? Are you crazy?

THE BARON. Oh—give her a wallop—that'll teach her to be less impertinent . . .

NASTYA. Just you try to touch me!

THE BARON. I shall!

SATINE. Stop! Don't insult her! I can't get the thought of the old man out of my head! [*Roars with laughter*] Don't offend your fellow-beings! Suppose I were offended once in such a way that I'd remember it for the rest of my life? What then? Should I forgive ? No, no!

THE BARON [*to* NASTYA].   You must understand that I'm not your sort . . . you—ah—you piece of dirt!

NASTYA. You bastard! Why—you live off me like a worm off an apple!

[*The men laugh amusedly.*]

KLESHTCH. Fool! An apple—?

THE BARON. You can't be angry with her—she's just an ass—

NASTYA. You laugh? Liars! Don't strike you as funny, eh?

THE ACTOR [*morosely*].   Give them a good beating!

NASTYA. If I only could! [*Takes a cup from the table and throws it on the floor*] That's what I'd like to do to you all!

THE TARTAR. Why break dishes—eh—silly girl?

THE BARON [*rising*].   That'll do! I'll teach her manners in half a second!

NASTYA [*running toward door*]. Go to hell!

SATINE [*calling after her*]. Hey! That's enough! Whom are you try-ing to frighten? What's all the row about, anyway?

NASTYA. Dogs! I hope you'll croak! Dogs! [*Runs out*]

THE ACTOR [*morosely*]. Amen!

THE TARTAR. Allah! Mad women, these Russians! They're bold, wilful; Tartar women aren't like that! They know the law and abide by it. . . .

KLESHTCH. She ought to be given a sound hiding!

THE BARON. The slut!

KLESHTCH [*testing the concertina*]. It's ready! But its owner isn't here yet—that young fellow is burning his life away . . .

SATINE. Care for a drink—now?

KLESHTCH. Thanks . . . it's time to go to bed . . .

SATINE. Getting used to us?

KLESHTCH [*drinks, then goes to his bunk*]. It's all right . . . there are people everywhere—at first you don't notice it . . . but after a while you don't mind. . . .

> [THE TARTAR *spreads some rags over his bunk, then kneels on them and prays.*]

THE BARON [*to* SATINE, *pointing at* THE TARTAR]. Look!

SATINE. Stop! He's a good fellow! Leave him alone! [*Roars with laughter*] I feel kindly to-day—the devil alone knows the reason why . . .

THE BARON. You always feel kindly when you're drunk—you're even wiser at such times . . .

SATINE. When I'm drunk? Yes—then I like everything—right—He prays? That's fine! A man may believe or not—that's his own affair—a man is free—he pays for everything himself—belief or unbelief—love—wisdom . . . a man pays for everything—and that's just why he's free! Man is—truth! And what is man? It's neither you nor I nor they—oh, no—it's you and they and I and the old man—and Napoleon—Mohammed—all in one! [*Outlines vaguely in the air the contour of a human being*] Do you understand? It's tremendous! It contains the be-ginning and the end of everything—everything is in man—and every-thing exists for him! Man alone exists—everything else is the creation of his hands and his brain! Man! It is glorious! It sounds—oh—so big! Man must be respected—not degraded with pity—but respected, re-spected! Let us drink to man, Baron! [*Rises*] It is good to feel that you are a man! I'm a convict, a murderer, a crook—granted!—When I'm out on the street people stare at me as if I were a scoundrel—they draw away from me—they look after me and often they say: "You dog! You humbug! Work!" Work? And what for? To fill my belly? [*Roars with laughter*] I've always despised people who worry too much about their bellies. It isn't right, Baron! It isn't! Man is loftier than that! Man stands above hunger!

THE BARON.　You—reason things out. . . . Well and good—it brings you a certain amount of consolation. . . . Personally I'm incapable of it . . . I don't know how. [*Glances around him and then, softly, guardedly*] Brother—I am afraid—at times. Do you understand? Afraid!— Because—what next?

SATINE.　Rot! What's a man to be afraid of?

THE BARON [*pacing up and down*].　You know—as far back as I can remember, there's been a sort of fog in my brain. I was never able to understand anything. Somehow I feel embarrassed—it seems to me that all my life I've done nothing but change clothes—and why? I don't understand! I studied—I wore the uniform of the Institute for the Sons of the Nobility . . . but what have I learned? I don't remember! I married—I wore a frock-coat—then a dressing-gown . . . but I chose a disagreeable wife . . . and why? I don't understand. I squandered everything that I possessed—I wore some sort of a grey jacket and brick-colored trousers—but how did I happen to ruin myself? I haven't the slightest idea. . . . I had a position in the Department of State. . . . I wore a uniform and a cap with insignia of rank. . . . I embezzled government funds . . . so they dressed me in a convict's garb—and later on I got into these clothes here—and it all happened as in a dream—it's funny . . .

SATINE.　Not very! It's rather—silly!

THE BARON.　Yes—silly! I think so, too. Still—wasn't I born for some sort of purpose?

SATINE [*laughing*].　Probably—a man is born to conceive a better man. [*Shaking his head*]—It's all right!

THE BARON.　That she-devil Nastka! Where did she run to? I'll go and see—after all, she . . . [*Exits; pause*]

THE ACTOR.　Tartar! [*Pause*] Prince! [THE TARTAR *looks round*] Say a prayer for me . . .

THE TARTAR.　What?

THE ACTOR [*softly*].　Pray—for me!

THE TARTAR [*after a silence*].　Pray for your own self!

THE ACTOR [*quickly crawls off the stove and goes to the table, pours out a drink with shaking hands, drinks, then almost runs to passage*]. All over!

SATINE.　Hey, proud Sicambrian! Where are you going?

[SATINE *whistles.* MIEDVIEDIEFF *enters, dressed in a woman's flannel shirt-waist; followed by* BUBNOFF. *Both are slightly drunk.*

BUBNOFF *carries a bunch of pretzels in one hand, a couple of smoked fish in the other, a bottle of vodka under one arm, another bottle in his coat pocket.*]

MIEDVIEDIEFF.   A camel is something like a donkey—only it has no ears. . . .

BUBNOFF.   Shut up! You're a variety of donkey yourself!

MIEDVIEDIEFF.   A camel has no ears at all, at all—it hears through its nostrils . . .

BUBNOFF [*to* SATINE].   Friend! I've looked for you in all the saloons and all the cabarets! Take this bottle—my hands are full . . .

SATINE.   Put the pretzels on the table—then you'll have one hand free—

BUBNOFF.   Right! Hey—you donkey—look! Isn't he a clever fellow?

MIEDVIEDIEFF.   All crooks are clever—I know! They couldn't do a thing without brains. An honest man is all right even if he's an idiot . . . but a crook must have brains. But, speaking about camels, you're wrong . . . you can ride them—they have no horns . . . and no teeth either . . .

BUBNOFF.   Where's everybody? Why is there no one here? Come on out . . . I treat! Who's in the corner?

SATINE.   How soon will you drink up everything you have? Scarecrow!

BUBNOFF.   Very soon! I've very little this time. Zob—where's Zob?

KLESHTCH [*crossing to table*].   He isn't here . . .

BUBNOFF.   Waughrr! Bull-dog! Brr-zz-zz!—Turkey-cock! Don't bark and don't growl! Drink—make merry—and don't be sullen!—I treat everybody—Brother, I love to treat—if I were rich, I'd run a free saloon! So help me God, I would! With an orchestra and a lot of singers! Come, every one! Drink and eat—listen to the music—and rest in peace! Beggars—come, all you beggars—and enter my saloon free of charge! Satine—you can have half my capital—just like that!

SATINE.   You better give me all you have straight away!

BUBNOFF.   All my capital? Right now? Well—here's a ruble—here's twenty kopecks—five kopecks—sun-flower seeds—and that's all!

SATINE.   That's splendid! It'll be safer with me—I'll gamble with it . . .

MIEDVIEDIEFF.   I'm a witness—the money was given you for safekeeping. How much is it?

BUBNOFF.   You? You're a camel—we don't need witnesses . . .

ALYOSHKA [*comes in barefoot*].   Brothers, I got my feet wet!

BUBNOFF.   Go on and get your throat wet—and nothing'll happen—you're a fine fellow—you sing and you play—that's all right! But it's too bad you drink—drink, little brother, is harmful, very harmful . . .

ALYOSHKA.   I judge by you! Only when you're drunk do you resemble a human being . . . Kleshtch! Is my concertina fixed? [*Sings and dances*]

> "If my mug were not so attractive,
>   My sweetheart wouldn't love me at all . . ."

Boys, I'm frozen—it's cold . . .

MIEDVIEDIEFF.   Hm—and may I ask who's this sweetheart?

BUBNOFF.   Shut up! From now on, brother, you are neither a policeman nor an uncle!

ALYOSHKA.   Just auntie's husband!

BUBNOFF.   One of your nieces is in jail—the other one's dying . . .

MIEDVIEDIEFF [*proudly*].   You lie! She's not dying—she disappeared—without trace . . .

[SATINE *roars.*]

BUBNOFF.   All the same, brothers—a man without nieces isn't an uncle!

ALYOSHKA.   Your Excellency! Listen to the drummer of the retired billygoats' brigade! [*Sings*]

> "My sweetheart has money,
>   I haven't a cent.
>   But I'm a cheerful,
>   Merry lad!"

Oh—isn't it cold!

[*Enter* ZOB. *From now until the final curtain men and women drift in, undress, and stretch out on the bunks, grumbling.*]

ZOB.   Bubnoff! Why did you run off?

BUBNOFF.   Come here—sit down—brother, let's sing my favorite ditty, eh?

THE TARTAR.   Night was made for sleep! Sing your songs in the daytime!

SATINE.   Well—never mind, Prince—come here!

THE TARTAR.   What do you mean—never mind? There's going to be a noise—there always is when people sing!

BUBNOFF [*crossing to* THE TARTAR].   Count—ah—I mean Prince—how's your hand? Did they cut it off?

THE TARTAR.   What for? We'll wait and see—perhaps it won't be necessary . . . a hand isn't made of iron—it won't take long to cut it off . . .

ZOB.   It's your own affair, Hassanka! You'll be good for nothing without your hand. We're judged by our hands and backs—without the pride of your hand, you're no longer a human being. Tobacco-carting—that's your business! Come on—have a drink of vodka—and stop worrying!

KVASHNYA [*comes in*].   Ah, my beloved fellow-lodgers! It's horrible outside—snow and slush . . . is my policeman here?

MIEDVIEDIEFF.   Right here!

KVASHNYA.   Wearing my blouse again? And drunk, eh? What's the idea?

MIEDVIEDIEFF.   In celebration of Bubnoff's birthday . . . besides, it's cold . . .

KVASHNYA.   Better look out—stop fooling about and go to sleep!

MIEDVIEDIEFF [*goes to kitchen*].   Sleep? I can—I want to—it's time—   [*Exit*]

SATINE.   What's the matter? Why are you so strict with him?

KVASHNYA.   You can't be otherwise, friend. You have to be strict with his sort. I took him as a partner. I thought he'd be of some benefit to me—because he's a military man—and you're a rough lot . . . and I am a woman—and now he's turned drunkard—that won't do at all!

SATINE.   You picked a good one for partner!

KVASHNYA.   Couldn't get a better one. You wouldn't want to live with me . . . you think you're too fine! And even if you did it wouldn't last more than a week . . . you'd gamble me and all I own away at cards!

SATINE [*roars with laughter*].   That's true, landlady—I'd gamble . . .

KVASHNYA.   Yes, yes. Alyoshka!

ALYOSHKA.   Here he is—I, myself!

KVASHNYA.   What do you mean by gossiping about me?

ALYOSHKA.   I? I speak out everything—whatever my conscience tells me. There, I say, is a wonderful woman! Splendid meat, fat, bones—over four hundred pounds! But brains—? Not an ounce!

KVASHNYA.   You're a liar! I've lot of brains! What do you mean by saying I beat my policeman?

ALYOSHKA.   I thought you did—when you pulled him by the hair!

KVASHNYA [*laughs*].   You fool! You aren't blind, are you? Why wash dirty linen in public? And—it hurts his feelings—that's why he took to drink . . .

ALYOSHKA.   It's true, evidently, that even a chicken likes vodka . . .

[SATINE *and* KLESHTCH *roar with laughter.*]

KVASHNYA.   Go on—show your teeth! What sort of a man are you anyway, Alyoshka?

ALYOSHKA.   Oh—I am first-rate! Master of all trades! I follow my nose!

BUBNOFF [*near* THE TARTAR's *bunk*]. Come on! At all events—we won't let you sleep! We'll sing all night. Zob!

ZOB. Sing—? All right . . .

ALYOSHKA. And I'll play . . .

SATINE. We'll listen!

THE TARTAR [*smiling*]. Well—Bubnoff—you devil—bring the vodka—we'll drink—we'll have a hell of a good time! The end will come soon enough—and then we'll be dead!

BUBNOFF. Fill his glass, Satine! Zob—sit down! Ah—brothers— what does a man need after all? There, for instance, I've had a drink— and I'm happy! Zob! Start my favorite song! I'll sing—and then I'll cry. . . .

ZOB [*begins to sing*]

"The sun rises and sets . . ."

BUBNOFF [*joining in*]

"But my prison is all dark. . . ."

[*Door opens quickly.*]

THE BARON [*on the threshold; yells*]. Hey—you—come—come here! Out in the waste—in the yard . . . over there . . . The actor—he's hanged himself. . . .

[*Silence. All stare at* THE BARON. *Behind him appears* NASTYA, *and slowly, her eyes wide with horror, she walks to the table.*]

SATINE [*in a matter-of-fact voice*]. Damned fool—he ruined the song . . . !

CURTAIN